"Yes, the Libecans Martini. It's basically a bigger, slightly richer take on a standard martini. It's delightful."

The waiter was sweet; he had a delicate voice and calm demeanour. I could tell he was a kind man.

"Both sound amazing. I'll try the first one and maybe the martini afterwards."

"Amazing. I'll get that fixed for you. Can I get you anything to eat?"

"Not just yet, thank you."

"No problem. My name's Ryan. If you need anything else don't hesitate to ask. My colleague, Brooke, is serving today as well if I'm not available at any point."

"Who?" My tone was abrupt.

"Brooke, she's the dark-haired girl by the bar." He pointed to a young girl, maybe twenty years of age, with a French plait and large circular glasses.

"Oh right, of course. I'm sorry."

Ryan looked at me with uncertainty, probably weighing whether I was tired or just peculiar. He smiled politely and headed back to the bar. It wasn't the first time I'd heard that name and automatically thought about her. My heart sank, as it so often did.

Immediately after she left, people told me, "Time is a healer", but I didn't believe it. Time brought distraction, and I learnt new ways to cope, but loss left a re-occurring reminder of what used to be. It could happen suddenly. I could be stood in a parking lot and see a car like the one she used to drive. I could be walking in the underground and see a woman with blonde hair loosely curled the way I loved hers, or I could be sat at my desk at work and I'd see her silhouette in the doorway. That's all it took, and the memories came flooding back.

Throwing myself into work was a welcome distraction, but I knew deep down the real reason I hadn't been on vacation for three years; I was scared to say it out loud or admit my fears to anyone. They would never understand.

Whenever I had a moment of weakness and broached the subject with Paula she didn't understand why I wasn't *over her*. Why hadn't I moved on with someone more suitable? Why did I keep the picture of her in the top drawer of my desk? They were all valid questions, but I couldn't explain.

I just had to be in England.

I had to be available.

Because—what if she came back?

CHAPTER TWO

The first-class cabin was sleek and modern. It felt a lot more intimate than the other two times I had flown first class—those times had been business expenditures and made no difference to my bank balance. I'd had the internal debate with myself as to whether it was worth the hefty price tag, but as soon as I stepped on the plane, I felt extremely comfortable with my decision. The flight attendant presented me with a glass of champagne. She smiled softly, greeting me with what seemed like a genuine message of welcome.

My aircraft was a 1-2-1 configuration, and I was a solo passenger, so I had opted for the seat against the window, three rows back from the front of the plane. The seats didn't line up, so it felt private. Once I eased into my stylish herringbone chair, I realised nobody could directly look into my little suite from across the aisle.

Perfect.

A different flight attendant brought a warm towel and a small ramekin of nuts, which could only mean one thing—no passengers with peanut allergies on the plane—even better. I was cocooned in what felt like a luxury sports car; it even had electronic controls so I could shift from lounge to bed mode with ease—*fancy*.

The amenity kit was a fine point. The soft black pyjamas looked even comfier than my casual business attire. I lay them to one side for a quick change in the bathroom at a later point. The small toiletry bag had all the necessities for a night away: moisturiser, toothpaste, deodorant, and numerous other travel sized products I would never use again. I rarely flew first class, so before the plane escaped to the skies I had already twisted the cap on the hand cream and lathered my fingers in the lavender infused lotion.

The inflight entertainment was a minefield. The screen brightly indicated it had over one thousand hours of blockbuster movies; within the first two minutes I'd seen five I wanted to watch. The noise-reducing headphones were a nice touch. By the time the plane was in the air I'd been offered my second drink, and the mood-lighting had kicked in. I was ready to hunker down and watch one too many Will Ferrell comedies, but first—I had some work to do.

I couldn't get over the fact that planes had Wi-Fi. As a child, I was under the illusion that if you so much as switched your electronic device on, the whole plane would combust and go down in a smoking ball of flames. Now, I could use my laptop, listen to music on my phone, or I could WhatsApp Paula a picture of my new pyjamas to make her jealous, all whilst watching a film I would only ever have the patience to watch on a plane.

I spent about ten minutes scrolling through social media with no real purpose. My laptop was open, poised, and ready for me to make valuable use of the time I had. Instead, I started searching for Brooke's name.

Is it something I did most days? Yes.

Was I proud of that? No.

For a moment my body froze. I held my breath. Maybe this time she would appear, but once again, I was left with crushing disappointment. No profile emerged. It had been that way since she left. It was a mutual agreement to block each other's access to socials. The truth was, I wanted to know what she was doing, where she was, who she was with; I wanted to have access to her life, but I understood why it was best I didn't.

Was she happy?

Did she have a career she enjoyed?

New friends?

A boyfriend?

The jealousy I felt at the possibility of her being with someone new caused severe nausea every single time I thought about her. I wasn't naive enough to believe she hadn't found someone else, but it didn't make the hurt any less severe. The question that kept me awake at night was—

Did she look for me too?

Paula kept telling me it was not knowing that made it difficult. I only wanted to know because I didn't know. If I had access to her, or if I still spoke with her, I would have moved on by now. Did I believe that? I'm not sure. I saw her point. It was the age old, *you always want what you can't have*, but it didn't mean I would want her less if I knew more about her life. The fear that consumed me was based on one overriding concern. What if I always wanted her?

I could see her brother's profile. **TomMJacobs** was his handle, and in his very modest description it said, *Too hot to handle! Just an English boy living in a Japanese world,* followed by a Japanese flag and a sushi emoji. It made me cringe.

His socials weren't of much interest to me. His feed consisted of pictures of him playing football, partying, and playing golf on a rooftop, which looked spectacular, but that was beside the point.

In the months after they left, Brooke appeared regularly on his feed. I felt like he was goading me. There was a photo of her trying authentic cuisine, another of

"Yep, Jake made me do it."

"Is Jake the cute bouncer with the buzz cut?"

I nodded. Clearly not cute enough for Beth to remember he practically carried her home on a night out about six years ago.

"Jake is the cute bouncer, yes. My point being, Rachael popped up on my suggestions." I chuckled. "I'm guessing she still can't decide which gender she prefers, huh?"

"She likes to keep her options open," Beth added.

"Can I safely say there is no real competition for Godmother then?"

"None at all." Beth smirked.

"Glad to hear it."

I infringed on her personal space with no remorse because she was my best friend. I placed my hand against her belly. "I've got you, kid. You stick with your auntie Holly, and you'll be just fine. Plus, when you're older I can get you out of trouble, pro bono of course."

"Let's hope it doesn't come to that." Beth smacked my hand away playfully.

"Yeah, but if it does. I've got you."

*

The drive back to Beth's apartment took almost an hour. We spoke about taking some day trips outside of Tokyo, getting away from the big city Beth was so accustomed to, and heading to the countryside. After extensive research, I'd learned Nikko was amazing to visit for its shrines and temples, and Kamakura was supposed to be a great place if you liked Buddha statues and Zen temples, which I did. Ever since Beth brought me a souvenir Buddha on her first trip back from Japan, I'd decided I just had to have one in every room. My latest addition sat on a shelf by the toilet. He's called *Nasam*, because, well, *Ratnasambhava* was too much of a mouthful.

Mount Fuji—the crème de la crème of mountains in Japan. Beth was adamant she didn't want to climb it, but I'd done my research, and you could take a bus partway up the mountain to experience the views. This was my fifth trip to Japan. There was still so much to see and do, and so little time to do it.

Beth's apartment had changed. A new driftwood style standing lamp hovered over the large cream sofa. Two matching circular tatami cushions on the opposite side of the coffee table kept the traditional Japanese style that Ren loved. There was a large gold framed mirror on the wall behind the sofa; that was new, and the scatter cushions were now a shade of yellow as opposed to green—Beth loved a theme change.

The spare bedroom looked exactly the same. The grey futon had already been pulled out and made up with a fresh set of linens. The wooden wardrobes had exposed rails for my clothes and shelves filled to maximum capacity with trinkets and photos of me and Beth amongst others. In the corner there was a small white desk with a leather office chair and a stack of paperwork nearing the ceiling. The apartment was small, so the spare room doubled as workspace when needed.

I dropped my shoulder by the door, allowing my bag to slide off and unintentionally sprawl its contents across the floor.

"Urgh, I'll deal with that later."

On the bed lay my favourite treats and the surprise I'd so carelessly spoilt. The tiniest little white babygrow had the words, *I love my auntie Holly*, spelt out across the front in pride colours. My eyes welled.

"Turn it over," Beth encouraged.

On the reverse there was a picture of a cartoon plane flying from the word Tokyo to London.

"I don't understand. What does this mean? Are you moving back home?" I grinned.

"It's an option." Beth leaned casually against the doorframe.

"You're kidding? Don't play with me, B. If you're moving back home, I'm about to become the happiest girl in the world." My smile was so wide my cheeks started hurting.

Beth laughed. She walked over to the small set of wooden drawers by the side of the bed and began neatly stowing my clothes.

"We spoke about it as soon as we found out. I've said to Ren since the beginning, if we were to have a child, I'd want to be closer to my parents. Ren isn't that close with his dad, and you know his mum passed away last year, so it makes sense. We would need help with the baby, and we don't have a lot of support here."

I slumped on the edge of the bed, watching Beth fold my clothes and aiding her by passing one T-shirt at a time. She liked to mother me, and I liked letting her.

"Wouldn't you miss Tokyo?"

She shrugged. "It was never supposed to be a permanent thing. I had this idea after university that I wanted to travel the world and experience different cultures whilst I was young. I thought I'd spend a couple of years here, then maybe move on to Thailand, then Brazil; I never expected to be here eight years later."

"You met the love of your life; that changes things."

"I did. And now we're having a baby." Her eyes widened.

I got up from my seated position and wrapped my arms around her torso, squeezing tightly around her chest because that's where I comfortably come up against her lanky frame.

"I would absolutely love it if you moved back home. You could all live with me until you find your feet. I'll babysit whenever you need. I'll be that supportive best friend that rubs your feet and buys you maternity pants and nursing bras because you're too embarrassed. You don't have to pay me a penny, and you can stay as long as you need." I muffled into the back of her soft black T-shirt.

"I know you would do all of those things, and that's why I love you." She turned towards me, pulling me in for a hug. "Nothing is off the table. We have a lot to figure out over these next few months."

I rested my head against her shoulder for a moment. The strands of her curly hair tickled my neck. The familiar smell of expensive perfume mixed with the strong scent of a shea butter body lotion she'd used since university filled my nostrils with a sense of belonging. My best friend was having a child—crazy.

"Enough about me. I've got a bottle of merlot chilling in the fridge."

I eyed her suspiciously.

"It's alcohol free of course." She threw her arms up in the air. "Just another thing a baby takes away. Apparently, I can't eat raw fish, coffee isn't great, and alcohol is frowned upon. How am I supposed to avoid raw fish in Japan? It's literally the sushi capital of the world." She sulked. "And I *really* love sushi."

"It's only nine months," I clarified. "Technically seven now. I'm sure you can survive."

*

The TV was playing *Attack on Titan* in the background. It was the one thing I'd never been able to connect with when it came to Japanese culture. Ren loved anime, so Beth had grown to enjoy it too. The non-alcoholic wine gave the illusion that I was drinking, but without the side-effects; I liked that. I opened the packet of Calbee crisps; that was a bad idea. I watched Beth judge me silently, so what if I liked crisps and wine together. Was that so odd?

"Don't you want me to make you something to eat?" Beth asked for the third time.

"Nope . . . I'm happy with these," I said through a mouthful of crunchy goodness.

When you fly for twelve hours through the night and are terrible at sleeping on a plane there is nothing else to do but eat to pass the time. My stomach was full to the brim with smoked salmon, potato gratin, slow cooked beef, and goat's cheese with chutney. The four-course meal was only bettered by the crisps I was currently eating. It was 7 p.m. Japanese time, which meant it was 11 a.m. in London, but my body felt like it was 3 a.m. and I'd stayed up four nights straight with someone smashing two tambourines against my head.

"How are you feeling being here?" Beth asked.

"Great. I always love coming to see you." I washed the crisps down with some more "wine".

Beth cringed.

"I don't mean that. I mean being in close proximity to you know who."

Oh, that.

midmorning snack before heading out. According to Beth, it was imperative we miss the noon lunch rush.

"Have I ever taken you to Tokyu Hands?" She asked.

"I don't think so."

"Oh no, I have done you a disservice. Let's go."

I had to stretch my legs to their full stride to keep up with Beth and her elongated pins. She dragged me towards a vertical green sign that scaled the side of a huge white building. The poster in the entrance window stated that Tokyu Hands was the place for the creative DIY enthusiast. The store was essentially a mixture of B&Q, Home Bargains, Boots, and The Range, all under one roof.

"This store changed my life. You will find things here you never knew you needed, life changing things."

Beth picked up a box with a label I couldn't read, but it had a picture of some toast on it.

"This is a ceramic toast steamer. I bought one a few months ago. It keeps the inside of your toast soft whist the outside gets crispy. Can you believe that?"

"Yes, I can believe that. It seems people will invent anything these days." The product resembled a small brown loaf of bread, or a brick, it was up for debate.

"I'll make you some toast tomorrow; you will eat your words."

She stuck out her tongue and ran towards the next fixture. If my mum's brain exploded, it would create this place. She was obsessed with anything quirky, gadgets, and craft items. She was semi-retired and spent the majority of her days doing paint by numbers or cross stitch.

I walked past an aisle purely dedicated to sticky notes. Yes, sticky notes! It was the most colourful ten metres I'd ever seen; I had to get the ones shaped like stilettos for Paula. I picked up a rubber keyboard cleaner in the shape of a duck and a green plastic plug that supposedly extends the life of lettuce and cabbage. These were things I had no use for, but the look of them intrigued me. I bought some erasers shaped like mochi, some glow sticks (not entirely sure why), and some paper soap—which is just genius. It was soap in the form of paper. It was pocket sized, so it could be carried around in my bag for all the times public restrooms ran out of soap. Genius.

Tokyu Hands was comprised of eight floors and contained every tool, gadget, toy, and random object you could ever find. I came out with a bag full of crap I didn't need, I'd convinced myself I did, and five thousand steps on my watch.

Do you know how long it takes to get around a place like that? Two hours! That's how long we spent in one store.

It was every Instagrammers dream.

*

Shibuya was the main hub of modern Tokyo and the perfect place to shop. In every direction I was overwhelmed by neon lights, bustling crowds, and intense outfit choices that made my attire look bleak in comparison. My standard Converse, oversized T-shirt, and my now busting canvas shopper bag were suitable for the weather, but the shoe choice was impractical. I was painfully aware I couldn't walk further than a mile in Converse without my little toe being severed—but I persisted. Maybe it was time to look for a new pair of trainers.

The stores were vast, and each had its own unique look and feel.

"I just love this place." Beth twirled in awe.

"It's something else."

Shibuya was the sight to see; it wasn't filled with temples or ancient shrines; it was known for its shopping and people watching. I recalled visiting on my first trip to Tokyo, but that was six years ago, so it felt like seeing it for the first time.

"The Scramble Square building wouldn't have been here the last time you came." Beth pointed towards a large all glass building towering above the famous pedestrian crossing. The majority of the glass windows were vertical, but the ones towards the bottom curved. When the sun caught the glass at a certain angle it gave off an optical illusion impression.

"Didn't we just go in there for Starbucks?" I asked. It looked familiar.

"Yes, but we didn't explore the other levels or the observation deck. There are fifteen floors of shops and restaurants." She beamed.

"After spending two hours in the Japanese version of Home Bargains, I could eat again."

My stomach grumbled; clearly, I'd worked up an appetite. The weight of the bag tugging on my shoulder became more noticeable the longer we walked.

The building was one giant sensory overload. I didn't know where to shop first, where to walk, or where to avoid. I wanted to sample everything. I started with a souvenir shop that specialised in handcrafted products. I found my mum a pair of posh panda chopsticks with gold tips. Weirdly, that was her one request.

Among the sweet shops on the first floor was a place called Mori Yoshida Paris, the famous patisserie made my mouth water the second we walked through the door. The warm sweet smell felt like I was inhaling heaven. Beth's nose practically touched the ceiling the more the scent aroused her senses.

"You look like a cartoon character. Like Jerry, when he floats through the air, the smell pulling him by his nostrils." I chuckled. *Tom & Jerry* had been my favourite programme growing up.

"Shut up."

The glass cabinets housed numerous creations in various shapes and sizes; they looked like works of art. We sampled as many pastries as the patient sales assistant would allow. I eventually settled on a cone shaped pastry that looked somewhat like an upside-down wasp's nest.

The sweet floor practically left me bankrupt. I purchased some cute macaroon-sized apple pastries, a chocolate caramel cookie sandwich, a strawberry classic shortcake, which looked like a mini layered cake with a little strawberry on top, and finally some salty rice balls.

"We can't stay on this floor any longer." I lifted the four different colourful bags and gave them a shake for effect. "What am I going to do with all this food?"

"You're the one with no willpower," Beth said whilst holding three bags of her own. "Don't worry, I'm sure I can help you eat them." She winked.

We made our way to the elevator. The tin box sped up to the fourteenth floor at lightning speed. You could tell it was a new building because there was no questionable screech or clangs of metal as the elevator came to a comfortable controlled stop. We purchased our tickets to the sky gallery and were directed to lockers to store our belongings.

"This was a great idea." My hands looked like the human equivalent of a pork loin from the handles cutting off my circulation. I bundled my bags into what should have been a reasonably sized locker, but not for someone who clearly had an addiction to sugar. I had to get two lockers. Beth smugly fit hers into one with a forceful closure.

We climbed into a different elevator. This one had built-in screens showcasing stars and light beams; it felt like a voyage into space. We were transported by escalators up to the huge panoramic observatory. The views were like nothing I'd ever experienced. I'd been to New York and seen the view from the Empire State Building. I'd even seen the view of London from the top of the Shard, but this was something spectacular.

"Unbelievable," I gasped.

"I know."

"Is this the first time you've been up here?" I asked.

"No, I came up with Ren when it first opened, but it was very brief; you know he's scared of heights." She rolled her eyes. She'd never been sympathetic to his fear.

"I bet he thanked you for that."

"I told him it wasn't that high, and it's not open air so it isn't scary."

"So, you lied." I laughed.

"Yep. I'm surprised he wants to have a child with me."

"Me too."

The artificial grass in the middle area of the open space offered the most unobstructed view. There were various ways to use the space: a mixture of solid white tables, waterproof sofas, and hammocks were strategically placed around the edges. When we saw a

The sto... ...hly
antici...

CHOOSE
Us

FROM BEST-SELLING LESBIAN ROMANCE AUTHOR
NICOLE SPENCER-SKILLEN

ALSO BY NICOLE SPENCER-SKILLEN

Choose Me

Are You Still Mine

If We Meet Again

If We Meet Again : The Wedding

If We Meet Again : The Choice

CHOOSE Us

*Copyright © 2023 Nicole Spencer-Skillen
All rights reserved.
No part of this book may be reproduced or used in any manner without the written permission of the copyright owner.*

This is a work of fiction. Names, characters, places, and incidents either are the product of the author's imagination or are used fictitiously. Any resemblance to actual people, living or dead, events or locales, is entirely coincidental.

Written in British English.

First Edition: May 2023

Edited by Laura Fortier

Cover by @bookcoversonline

To my awesome readers:

Remember that time I left the first novel on a cliff-hanger? Whoops. I'm sorry about that, or am I? Ha-Ha. I can't promise there won't be more cliff-hangers, but I can promise there will always be more books. Thank you for sticking by me, your unwavering support means the world.

Nicole

CHAPTER ONE

Did I always want to be a lawyer?—Yes.
Did I regret my profession?—Only 25 percent of the time.
Today was one of those days.
It was Thursday, and I'd clocked hours above and beyond a regular working week. Law was anything but a nine-to-five job, and rarely did I have time for lunch, unless it was a business lunch, then I took full advantage. There had to be some *perks*.
The reality of my daily routine was a far cry from the dramatised portrayals on television. When I watched Reese Witherspoon boss the courtroom in *Legally Blonde*, I didn't see how hard it could be. I've never solved a case by using my knowledge of a permanent wave hairstyle, but I don't deny the knowledge has been relevant before.
I naively figured all I had to do was gain the relevant legal knowledge—basically, don't waste my years at university—and make sure I thoroughly study the case at hand, and somehow all the expansive law terms and key witness testimonies would fall into my lap, making the courtroom part a piece of cake.
How wrong I was.
I turned thirty this year; with that came a whole new decade, a whole new breadth of knowledge to learn, and wrinkles—yep, those were appearing in hordes like a small army trying to break down the walls of my face. I found myself clicking on the anti-aging article that

popped up on my phone and examining face creams for SPF and collagen. There were a variance of remedies and tips, but every article stated I should protect my skin from the sun and get lots of sleep. The first I could hypothetically achieve; the second was an impossibility.

I reached for my briefcase and shoved the majority of the contents of my desk inside. I glanced at the clock; it was 5 p.m. already? How did that happen?

"Crap."

I checked my plane ticket on my phone for the fifth time that day. My flight to Japan would depart in less than three hours. I'd barged into the office at 7 a.m. balancing my scalding hot chai latte in one hand and my ponderous briefcase in the other, with the intention of skipping through the clearly labelled exit door two or three hours later. I've discovered in my adult life, my expectations are often too high, unrealistic, or altogether forlorn, but I tried, and that had to count for something.

Early mornings at West & Barnes were my most productive time of day. The office wasn't officially open for business. The faint sound of the coffee machine and my fingers tapping against the laptop keys was heavenly. Rarely did I have early calls; there were no scheduled appointments, and best of all, no Grace from legal questioning why I thought it was appropriate to take a client to lunch at Bob Bob Ricard's. Their steak served with Siberian sturgeon caviar sealed the deal. You had to speculate to accumulate; Grace did not agree.

After ten hours of work, I still had correspondence to reply to, new information to read regarding upcoming court cases, and messages from attorneys or their paralegals seeking updates on pending cases to respond to. Luckily, the flight to Japan would take twelve hours, giving me plenty of time to continue working—if I ever got on the flight.

Paula stormed into the office just as I forced the metal clasp on my briefcase into place, the familiar clipping sound usually signified the end of a long day, but today was far from over.

"Oh good, you're still here." Her fiery red hair matched the colour of her skin; she was visibly out of breath.

"Are you okay?" I chuckled.

"Yes, have you seen the article?"

"The one about anti-aging?"

She rolled her eyes. "I'll take that as a no." Paula pulled her phone from her pocket and began typing away.

"*The Guardian* released an article about the Mason/Russo trial; someone sent me the link. Hold on . . . Here." Paula removed her thick framed glasses from her hair and placed them delicately on the end of her nose. "It says, 'Defence Barrister Holly Garland is sharp and thinks on her feet. She brutally unmasked the defence's witness, Rebecca Gilden, for the liar she is. The trial of Lance Mason and Natalia Russo concluded after two weeks in court. The jury deliberated for thirteen hours before unanimously finding Lance Mason guilty of second-degree murder. It was a fierce encounter between the two women, but Garland came out on top'."

The words escaped Paula's mouth in one long breathless spiel.

"That sounds great." I reached for my phone, shoving it in my pocket along with my house keys and a packet of chewing gum—the essentials.

"Is that it?"

"What do you want me to say?" I shrugged.

"At least be a little enthusiastic. Daniel Shard is a detestable and extremely unpleasant man with absolutely nothing good to say about women. He once said, and I quote, 'Being a lawyer is a male profession'."

"That was two decades ago." Daniel Shard was very much an asshole, the biggest, most controversially derogative asshole, but I liked to wind Paula up anyway because she used to date him in high school.

"Regardless, he's still a chauvinistic pig who basically said you're like the queen of the courtroom."

"Did he use the word queen? I'm not sure he did." Any enthusiasm towards the article diminished sharply after hearing it. The applause didn't appeal the same anymore.

"Oh, piss off." Paula dramatically slapped her phone case shut and shoved it deep within her trouser pocket. "You used to love this sort of thing. What's happened to you?"

Paula was right; my wall had previously been filled with newspaper articles from my biggest case wins. They were a reminder of how far I'd come, and probably my justification for working double the hours deemed appropriate for a work/life balance. The praise and gratification were shamefully what fuelled me for the first several years of my career.

In the last two years I'd changed. *Heartbreak* changed me. It was a word thrown around with ease, but I had never felt its true power until Brooke left. If my soul were a wall, that event crumbled it into pebble sized pieces in the middle of an old warzone, and there were no signs of re-building.

I didn't use the word heartbreak lightly anymore. The tightening in my chest was still there, as a reminder of the breathless pain and the excruciating weight of a love lost. I could break down at any moment, I was living on an emotional edge. Eventually I had to release the hurt, let it go, and let it fade away like a bad dream. I'd lost the person I thought I would spend the rest of my life with. The loss made me realise love wasn't all it was cracked up to be.

That's what I wanted to say. Instead I said, "I don't know. I'm trying to be less . . ."

It wasn't often words failed me, but it had been happening a lot lately. It was time for a vacation.

"Career obsessed?" Paula asked.

"No."

"Superficial?"

I scowled. "No . . ."

"Narcissistic?"

"No." I raised my eyebrow. "Wait, what? That's how you see me? A career obsessed, superficial, narcissistic prick?"

"I never said the prick part." Paula smirked. "You're not really those things, well maybe sometimes, but not so much anymore." Paula grinned and flicked aside her long red fringe as though she hadn't just insulted me.

"Good to know." I did one last sweep of my desk. Everything confidential was dealt with or locked away to be dealt with on my return. "I was going to say, I'm trying to be less tied down by other people's opinions of me."

"Huh." Paula leaned against the doorframe.

"What?" I grabbed my coat from the rack, tucked it between the handles of my briefcase, and I was ready to go. It was July, so a jacket wasn't necessary, but in true British fashion the weather forecast predicted clouds with a chance of rain between the hours of—pretty much all day.

"I just figured it was ... Y'know?" She nodded towards my chest area.

"No, I don't know?"

"Y'know ..." She waved back and forth with her hand.

"No, I still don't know." Her expression changed to one of sympathy, which only meant one thing. "Will you just spit it out?"

"You've sort of been a shadow of your former self since Brooke left," Paula said softly.

"That was almost two years ago, Paula." Not that it mattered, but I'd had to sell it and pretend everything was okay. I didn't have time to get caught up in my feelings. "It's a thing of the past."

It wasn't, not really. I never spoke about Brooke anymore; it didn't take much for me to reminisce. A photo on social media often sparked an hour-long stalk of all her social platforms. The toilets in the underground brought back a memory so clear I could taste her lips on mine, and even six months after she'd left, just seeing Ashleigh at reception wearing the same coat Brooke had been so fond of brought a tear to my eye. Thankfully, two years passed, and Ashleigh purchased a new coat. The triggers were everywhere, but with time and numerous sexual partners they had become easier to ignore, but they never disappeared. They lingered unwanted and provoking.

"If you say so." Paula shrugged. "Anyway, are you excited for Japan?"

"I will be once I get on the plane. Walk with me to the elevator?"

Paula grabbed my suitcase and began wheeling it across the hall; it was an amusing sight in six-inch heels.

"Did you schedule an appointment with Mrs. Byker?" I asked.

"Yes. Next Tuesday at 2 p.m."

Good.

"Has the assailant's lawyer in the Wilde case gotten back to you with the information we asked for?"

"Yes, got that. I'll review it this afternoon and arrange a meeting if anything is unclear."

I nodded.

"And you're okay to look after my emails? You can call me if there's anything urgent."

"Yes, absolutely."

I sighed—relief.

"You're acting like this is the first time you've been away. I've got this under control, don't worry."

"I haven't been anywhere for almost three years."

"I'm aware." Paula rolled her eyes. "I've been trying to force you to take a holiday since . . . you know when."

Since the girl I loved left me with a goodbye letter and flew halfway around the world to live her life under the strict guidance of her controlling homophobic father?

I'm not bitter at all.

My heart dropped every time I thought about her, which had been a lot since she'd left. Of all the places she could've moved it had to be Japan. It was the one place I visited repeatedly. My best friend Beth was excited to see me, and I was crippled with anxiety.

"Uh huh."

"What are you most excited to do when you get there?" Paula slammed her fingers on the elevator down arrow.

"I've seen quite a lot already, but I've never climbed Mount Fuji. The climbing season is July to September so it's perfect." I used to go to Japan with my ex, Danielle, and she could rarely have time off during the summer months, so I'd only been to Japan in the summer once before.

"Make sure you take lots of pictures if you do! I don't know if I've mentioned it before, but I've never been to Japan."

"Once or twice." I smirked.

"I'm lucky if Jeremy wants to leave the damn country." She sulked.

The elevator clinked and crashed as it zoomed into place. The arrow disappeared, and the red light flashed 3.

"He surprised you with a trip to Scotland last month," I said.

"It's not Dubai though, is it?" She propped the door open with her hand as I shuffled inside; the elevator was empty.

"You're hard to please." I chuckled.

"You wouldn't expect Michelle Pfeiffer to be happy staying in a dingy two-bedroom cottage in the middle of Scotland surrounded by sheep and smelling like pig shit, would you?" Once she'd forcefully rolled my suitcase into the lift, she placed her hands on her hips.

"You're not Michelle Pfeiffer! For starters you're about 250 million pounds poorer."

"Erm ... How do you know I don't own this law firm. I could be on that show—What's it called now?—*Fake Boss*? *Poor Boss*?"

"*Undercover Boss*?"

"That's it!" She whacked my arm excitedly. "I knew it had boss in it."

"I think I'll rest easy knowing you're not the undercover boss when you don't even know the name of the show."

"It might be part of my plan." She was holding the elevator doors open; they shoved her once, twice, before jutting back into the frame.

"Paula, I love you, but I have to go." My watch is telling me I should've left fifteen minutes ago.

"Right, sorry. You've got a plane to catch. Let me know when you land safely. Don't do anything I wouldn't do, and take lots of pictures. I need to live my life vicariously through you because Jeremy is a boring bastard."

"Thank you." She stepped back to let the doors close. The last thing I saw were her eyebrows jolting upwards and her hand reaching out. "Don't forget to email about—"

And she was gone.

The mirror on the left of the elevator did me no favours. I wished I had a time lapse of my years at West & Barnes. My life would flash before my eyes with one photo from every morning and every evening in the elevator mirror. I was certainly more worn out come the end of the day, as could be seen when the little cracks around my eyes appeared; they were covered so delicately by concealer in the morning but had nowhere to hide come evening. My mum tells me they're just laugh lines, and Paula pointed out they'll be a lot worse when I'm her age, but that didn't stop me looking at the brochure for the aesthetics boutique around the corner.

Today my eyes looked drawn and duller than normal. I was tired, I guess. My life had been work, some more work, and even more work, for the past two years. Work had become my coping mechanism. My brown hair looked okay. I'd treated it to a cut and blow two days prior, so it wasn't as tatty as it had been. My stylist advised me to purchase a strengthening conditioner; I took offence, but split ends were no joke.

Every day I put on a smile and pretended not to notice the sadness behind my eyes. As I observed my reflection in the mirror, I saw it. Part of my life was never the same after Brooke left, and I wasn't sure it ever would be.

*

The airport felt more crowded than usual. The perks of flying first class allowed me to skip the queues and head straight to the dedicated check-in desk; much to everyone else's dismay. I felt embarrassed, but only temporarily. Once I was through the fast-track security and into The Concorde Room I felt comfortable.

The room was filled with business men and women. Luckily, I'd not changed from my work attire, so I didn't feel out of place. I'd gone for my black jersey suit that morning because it was unstructured and felt like wearing a tracksuit; coupled with a pair of trainers and a white T-shirt, it was my textbook "smart/casual" look. I had a hoodie in my backpack to change into on the plane once the dreaded air-conditioning kicked in. I took a seat in a discreet booth in the corner; within seconds a waiter arrived.

"Hello, welcome to The Concorde Lounge. Can I get you something to drink, Miss?"

I quickly scanned the menu, but the choices were unusual. "What do you recommend?"

"The Barton cocktail is my favourite. It contains gin, elderflower, dandelion and burdock, soda, and rosemary. It's sublime."

It sounded interesting. "Do you have a martini?"

her posing with her father, and one with her arm casually slung around the shoulders of a young Japanese man. He was head to toe in football gear, so I assumed he was one of Tom's friends. It was the second photo in a photo dump entitled, *Mad weekend*, followed by a tongue face emoji.

A month or so later he dedicated a post to Brooke for her birthday. It showcased pictures from their childhood up to a recent one of them lounging by a pool; again, there was a third man in the photo. He sat close enough to Brooke to make me take a second and a third look. I analysed the photo like it was a key piece of evidence in a murder trial. Eventually, it drove me insane, and I blocked her brother too—at least for a short period of time. Curiosity got the better of me eventually.

Brooke lived approximately an hour away from Beth in a place called Yokohama. I knew that because we'd had a brief conversation the week after she arrived. Trying to keep a conversation *brief* with the potential love of your life was more difficult than I'd anticipated. I used the word *potential* in the hope maybe there was still someone out there for me, and I hadn't lost my one and only chance of happiness, because, well, that thought was soul-destroying.

Beth lived in a neighbourhood called Hatagaya, just outside of Tokyo. It was a relaxed area with coffee shops, small bars, friendly faces, and a lot of Japanese language I couldn't read. The two-bedroom apartment she shared with her boyfriend Ren was situated in a quiet block of apartments not far from the train line, so access was easy when we wanted to explore.

My phone pinged, and a message from Beth dropped down at the top of my screen.

It read:

Beth
I CANNOT wait to see you!! Hurry up and get here. I got all your favourite things ready. Love you xoxo

Three photos followed: Alfort biscuits in white chocolate, Calbee potato chips, and Puccho soft candy chews in grape flavour—my favourite. The, *xoxo*, had stuck since our obsessive *Gossip Girl* days back at university—we shipped Blake and Penn an unhealthy amount until their demise in 2010.

I have experimented with many different sweet snacks during my visits to Japan, but the process of narrowing down to my ultimate favourite happened over numerous visits and food filled packages sent through the post.

The last time I saw Beth in person was eleven months ago. She came to England for a stint during the summer, and with it brought three weeks of childlike behaviour, more coffee trips than a human should take, and many drunken nights. I'd introduced her to Francesca.

Francesca was an Italian exchange student studying for her MA at the University of London. We dated for just over two months. She was beautiful, endearing, and quite sweet. Her accent was the most velvety inviting accent I'd ever heard. It was seductive and calm. I will never deny I enjoyed her company. She was easy to talk to, she listened, and she understood my need for casual encounters.

Francesca possessed all the distinctive characteristics of an Italian woman, from olive skin, to high cheekbones, to dark hair, and the most intense gaze I have ever seen. She was a dream, but it didn't take her long to figure out she wasn't my dream. My mind was reserved for only one person—it still is.

*

My thirtieth birthday weekend was the last time I saw Beth, and Francesca for that matter. I insisted I didn't want a big elaborate celebration. I wanted to say a quiet goodbye to my twenties and hello to a new fun-filled decade.

My mum didn't allow that. She went ahead and did the complete opposite, but that was my mum. She assumed everything I said was a cryptic clue in a crossword puzzle. On reflection I should have asked for a giant party with giraffes, large gavel shaped balloons, and a baby elephant. I would've ended up with a quiet meal at our local Italian with the waiters bellowing "Happy Birthday" across the restaurant and a small piece of chocolate cake with one candle.

I asked for a quiet gathering and ended up face first in the wheelie bin at the side of my apartment. It had been Beth's job to remove me from the house and keep me distracted for at least two hours whilst my parents set up. Beth was terrible at keeping secrets, so I knew within ten minutes of leaving I would return to what looked like the inside of a clown's brain.

The decorations were even more extravagant than I'd anticipated. The theme was black and gold. The cake had been made professionally in the shape of a law book with a gavel hitting the thirty into the cake. It was the single coolest thing to come from flour and eggs. My family and friends made the trip from Newquay. Several people from work came too, and for the first fifteen minutes I felt overwhelmed by the sheer amount of love and well wishes.

One minor incident turned the party on its head. You see, my mum was never good at leaving things alone. She had to meddle. Her intentions were good, but she had to involve herself in things that didn't concern her.

"Holly, sweetheart, come here." She waved me over from the kitchen. Her hair was freshly coloured, with a hint of strawberry blonde, a look her hairdresser insisted would make her ten years younger.

"Your hair looks great today."

"Thanks honey. I curled it myself. Janine, you know Janine, right? Well, she uses this curling wand thing. It's so easy to use, and your curls last for hours. I did think about getting you one for your birthday, but I know you don't really spend time curling your hair, so I figured it would be a waste. I almost bought one for Danielle—"

Danielle was my ex-girlfriend. Granted, I was with her for eight years, but she hadn't been in my life for over three years at this point, and she still occasionally slipped into conversation. It was a habit, and I didn't blame my mum for that. She'd spent eight Christmases, eight birthdays, and eight of every other family occasion and holiday including Danielle. It was going to take a while for her to not be mentioned in conversation. She never mentioned Brooke, maybe because to her that relationship was fleeting. She didn't see the lasting effects, and I didn't care to show them. It was easier that way.

"Whoops. Sorry." She chuckled. "Anyway, I know I gave you your gift already, but I got you something else."

She pulled a black leather satchel from underneath the kitchen island. A big gold bow graced the front; it looked expensive.

"The last time I came here I noticed your work bag was looking a little worse for wear, and the other week I went shopping and saw this bag in the window at Selfridges. I nearly fell on the floor when they told me the price, but it is a big birthday, and I thought it would be perfect for you."

"You shouldn't have. It's beautiful, but so expensive Mum. You've already spent enough." I edged closer to observe the details.

"Don't be silly." She waved me off, and then turned into a sales assistant. "The woman I spoke to said it's great for business men or women—it's unisex, which I thought was fantastic because I think gender identities have transformed significantly, and you shouldn't feel like you have to buy from the men's section if you're a man and the ladies' section if you're a woman." My jaw hit the floor. I glanced at Beth who was trying hard not to crack a smile. I am not entirely sure when my mum became such a queer ally, but she'd clearly read an article on one of her obsessively long Facebook scrolls.

"It's got this little latch here, inside there's all these different pockets; one specifically designed to put your pens in—I got you a new pen by the way. There are a few zip pockets too and it even comes with a spare strap, which I thought was great considering your last one snapped." She went through each compartment one by one. "I even transferred all your things from your old bag into this one."

My smile faded.

"Wait, you did what?" I pulled the bag frantically from her grasp. I searched through every compartment looking for the letter.

"Where's my old bag, Mum?"

"I threw it out. It was in terrible condition." She shrugged.

"You chucked my old bag in the bin? What the hell, Mum? Brooke got me that bag." The last part came out as a high-pitched squeal. The sheer panic caused my breathing to deepen; my chest felt tight.

I need to find the letter.

"I'm sorry honey. I thought you'd be happy with a new bag."

"Where is . . . In my old bag there was a little zip compartment hidden inside another. Did you empty that? I can't find the . . ." I searched every inch of the bag.

Beth remained silent.

My mum placed her hand softly on my shoulder.

"Holly, what are you looking for?"

"I need to find my old bag. There's a letter, and . . . I have to find it Mum, okay? You can't just touch my things Mum; that's not fair." I stormed out of the apartment, narrowly missing Francesca at the entrance to the kitchen.

"Holly, wait—" my mum called.

In my adrenaline-fuelled outburst I'd not even noticed Francesca's presence. I ran down the stairs, taking two at a time and made a beeline to the side of the building where the communal bins where located. I desperately searched the first one—nothing. The second covered my hands in a combination of disgusting food related liquids merged to create a fluid that I'm sure would strip paint—bin juice. Finally, the third bin revealed my brown leather satchel sat miserably between two large bin bags.

I pulled the back out and slumped back against the brick wall. I opened the hidden compartment to reveal the letter.

Brooke's letter.

It was folded four ways and was crinkled and torn slightly from the number of times I'd read it. The bag was sentimental; it was one of the only things I had left of her. Despite the need for a replacement, I'd persevered with it for many months, hiding it from sight when I attended meetings so people wouldn't think my work was a reflection of my work accessory—shabby and tattered.

I opened the letter the same way I always did, carefully pulling at each corner, conscious not to cause any more damage. The reality was I could recite every single word if I needed to, and most days I did. It wasn't something to be proud of, but it confirmed the depth in which my heart still yearned for her. Maybe, Brooke never understood the magnitude of her words or how literally I would take them.

I hold out hope, maybe, one day, things could be different.

Francesca approached a moment later. She looked exquisite in a green button through shirt dress; its beige belt pulled the dress in at the waist accentuating her curvy figure. I was there covered in bin juice and clutching a tattered letter like it was worth a colossal sum—To me it was.

"Are you okay?" she asked.

I nodded. My breathing had returned to a normal rhythm pretty quickly.

Francesca's eyes glistened. It made my stomach drop. "I don't think I can do this anymore, Holly," she said softly.

"What do you mean?"

"I knew when I started this with you that you were still hung up on her, and you were honest with me. You told me how you felt. You told me you weren't sure if you could get over her, so I'm not blaming you." She sighed. "I guess I thought it would be like any other heartbreak; you think you can't move on, but you do. I thought with time I could make you think differently. You would see there was something other than her, something better."

I climbed to a standing position; it wasn't my finest moment slumped by the side of a dust bin. I was accustomed to Francesca's accent by that point. I was aware of the way she blended "th" and the elongation of double consonants and the way she said better like "better". Her accent was so attractive to me.

"I am over her . . . I just didn't want my mum to throw my bag out." I smiled, but she wasn't foolish. I knew she would see straight through my lies.

"You didn't want her to throw the letter out, you mean." She pointed towards the small piece of paper in my hand. Did she know about the letter? I didn't recall telling her.

"Don't look so surprised. You're not great at keeping secrets. Do you remember the first night I stayed over at your apartment? The next day I came down to the kitchen and I saw you reading something; you quickly folded it away and put it in your bag. You said it was 'work stuff'. I could tell you were lying, but it wasn't my place. Then, I saw you do it again about a week later. I was curious, so I looked at the piece of paper in your bag." Francesca shrugged as though that wasn't a complete invasion of my privacy.

"You went through my stuff?"

"I know I shouldn't have, but I had to see for myself. I didn't read it. Once I saw it was a letter from Brooke, I put it back. Since then, I've known this thing between us had a time limit." Francesca walked towards me, planted a kiss on my forehead, and turned to walk away.

"Francesca, I'm sorry." I wanted to say more. I wanted to want her the way she wanted me. I wanted to be over Brooke; I really did. I wanted the beautiful Italian woman before me with the moonlight glistening around her like a halo to be the one that finally helped me move on. "I do really like you . . . I just . . ."

"Wrong timing." She wrapped her arms across her chest. "Take care of yourself, Holly." The flowing material of her dress lingered as she rounded the corner, and I hated myself for losing her.

Beth came to find me and ushered me inside. My mother apologised profusely, and the evening continued, but it didn't feel like a celebration. After one too many glasses of champagne I loosened up, but something was missing; or should I say, *someone*.

I didn't speak to Francesca much after that. We exchanged the occasional text, and about a month ago she asked for some legal advice for her friend, but we found ourselves in a strange situation. Admittedly, there were too many feelings for us to be friends, but not enough to be something more.

*

Two hours into the flight, a female attendant approached me. Her badge informed me her name was Sarah. She had a sweet aura, was smiley and polite, but not in a fake way, and she seemed like she genuinely loved her job. She made the trip bearable.

"Would you like another cocktail, Miss Garland?" She gestured towards my empty glass.

"I would love another Highland Sling please." It was my third cocktail of the flight so far, and my favourite. The raspberry liqueur, apple juice, and whiskey was a combination I never thought I'd enjoy. My head started to feel drowsy. The lapse in time from my brain wanting to say something to my mouth forming the words was growing in length. It was almost time to go down for the night.

"Of course. Coming right up."

She was back a few minutes later with the tall glass. The rim was infused with a hint of sugar and a slice of apple for decoration.

"Can I get you anything else, Miss Garland?"

"I don't think so, but I am almost ready to get some sleep I think, if you could help me get the bed ready?"

"Of course. I will be right back with the linens."

"Thank you so much."

I closed my laptop and adjusted the pull-out table that acted as a workspace. In packing away my laptop and notebook I felt a moment of weakness. I removed the letter from my satchel. It had been almost six months since I last looked at it. I tried desperately not to dwell on the words, but I wondered if Brooke did the same, or if she even still had my letter.

I was doing well until the bartender's name at the airport threw me. Maybe I was naive to think flying to Japan wouldn't make me obsess over her. I was about to be the closest I had been to Brooke in two years, but I could get through it. I could survive my two weeks in Japan the same way I survived the two years without her.

I could get over her.

Maybe, I already had.

But—It couldn't hurt to read the letter one more time.

Dear Holly,

I have started this letter a thousand times . . .

CHAPTER THREE

Speedy clearance through immigration and customs at Narita International Airport was exactly what I needed after stepping off a luxurious but long twelve-hour flight. According to the captain we'd managed to shave twenty-three minutes off the arrival time thanks to some heavy tail winds, which meant I was earlier than anticipated.

The automatic doors burst open into the arrivals hall, and the chaos began. There were people frantically buying train tickets, family members embracing each other, and several people waving leaflets in the face of the poor woman working at the information counter. I stalled for a moment, I searched for Beth, but I was unable to locate her.

Instead, my eyes observed a young embracing couple who, in the midst of a crowded hall, were completely unwavering. The world moved around them, but I watched them remain completely still, solid in their joint endeavour—to be with one another. I wanted to know their story. I wanted to feel what they felt in that moment. It seemed as though the world around them had no meaning or context. I wanted to feel what it was like to be in a world where love prevailed.

Then, a man with four suitcases almost sent them flying like two heart-shaped bowling balls across the polished marble floor. I snapped back to reality. I spotted a curly brown-haired girl bobbing and weaving her way through the crowds. At five feet and eleven inches, Beth was hard to miss; it had to be her. She rounded the final human shaped obstacle, and there she was, all blue-eyed and refreshed.

"Holly!" She threw her arms around my neck. My hand luggage fell to the floor, and my complimentary pyjamas I'd been carrying around like a first-class first-timer went down with it. I embraced her vice-like grip, sinking into the space between her shoulder and her neck like a baby kangaroo waiting to snuggle down in its mum's pouch. Beth felt like a piece of home, and to me there was nothing better than a piece of home when I was so exhausted. One glimpse at my reflection in the toilet mirror before we disembarked the plane made me concerned that my eyes might possibly sink so far into my head I'd be left with black holes.

Beth squeezed tighter and tighter until I feared my neck might snap.

"Beth. I can't breathe."

She eased off slightly, "I'm not ready to let go yet."

"I've missed you," I said.

"I've missed you more."

When I pulled back, she reached down for my suitcase. Her hair was bouncier than normal, or was it the colour? The length? Something was different. "Is your hair shorter?"

"Yes, do you love it?" She flicked her head left and then right. Her curls were elastic almost.

"I do." There was something else; it wasn't just the hair. Beth was radiating a different kind of energy.

"You look . . ."

"Pretty?" She grinned.

"No . . ."

"Model-like?" She posed with her hand on her hip.

"No . . ."

"Pfft—way to make a girl feel good." She sulked and grabbed my complimentary pyjamas from the floor.

"Obviously you're both of those things, but that's not it, you look . . . glowing." I said it suspiciously, "Which means one of two things, you've either invested in a new skin care routine that's working wonders for you, if so I'd like the details, or you're pregnant." The guilty look on Beth's face indicated the latter.

"You're PREGNANT!" I yelled.

"Shh, Jesus Hol! The whole of Tokyo doesn't need to know." She dragged me by the arm away from the crowds and towards the exit.

"Why the hell didn't you tell me? How long have you known? Is it Ren's? Does Ren know? Was it planned? How far along are you?" I had so many questions. My head was about to explode.

"Woah, woah, woah. Please slow down." She placed her hand on my shoulder. "I'll explain on the drive home, I promise."

"But, wait . . ."

She was gone, leaving me with a large suitcase and no choice but to chase my newly pregnant best friend who speed walked faster than I could run.

"B . . . I need answers."

*

The second all four wheels of the car hit the expressway I jumped straight in. I couldn't take it any longer.

"How long?" I started off lightly.

"Eight weeks," Beth said.

"Eight weeks?" I stared at her in utter disbelief. "You've been pregnant for eight weeks, and you didn't tell me?"

"Technically I only found out at week five, so I only kept it a secret from you for the last three weeks, if that makes you feel any better." She smiled coyly.

"It doesn't." I adjusted my seatbelt so I could sit sideways and stare at her unnecessarily. "Is it Ren's?"

"Of course it's Ren's. Do you think I'd cheat on Ren and not tell you? As if!" She rolled her eyes.

"Oh yeah, it's not like you didn't tell me you were pregnant or anything," I said matter-of-factly.

Beth side-eyed me. That was my first warning. Pregnant or not, she could beat me hands down in a play fight. Her legs were as lengthy as stilts but with the strength of Tyson Fury; it was a dangerous combination.

"I wanted to tell you in person. I have a surprise at the apartment for you. You weren't supposed to guess the second you stepped off the plane with your crazy pregnancy-detecting superpowers."

"Sorry, it's a gift. Did I tell you about the time I guessed my client's wife was pregnant in the middle of a trial? She was only in the early stages, but he'd had a vasectomy, so it blew the whole case wide open. I also guessed that my aunt Hilda's daughter was pregnant before she officially wanted to tell everyone. Maybe I should just keep these things to myself in future."

"Yeah, maybe." Beth chuckled.

"I'm assuming it wasn't planned? At no point in recent years have you told me you want kids; actually, you told me teaching them was enough to put you off for life."

Heck, Beth teaching them was enough to put me off kids for life. Only an unbreakable, earth-shattering, blood-sharing bond can make anyone think cleaning up baby puke and packages of green coloured faeces for years on end is worth it.

"That still stands. It wasn't planned, but when I told Ren he was really excited. His friends have started to have children, and it's making him jealous. He feels like he's missing out, so he's happy."

"And you? Are you excited? Because you don't seem so excited."

At all.

"I am and I'm not. I hear mixed views. People have kids and say they wouldn't change it for the world, but I have this fear of losing my identity and becoming just a mum, y'know? Plus, I teach kids all day every day. Do I really want my own to contend with when I get home?" Beth gripped the steering wheel tightly. She manoeuvred from lane to lane with a fierce determination. "I don't know; it's just a lot to think about isn't it."

"I think you'll make a great mum. Yes, your priorities might change, but I'm sure they'll change for the better. I don't know anyone who's said they wished they didn't have their child." There was a woman I'd defended a few years back who was adamant she'd drop them off at school and never pick them up again if they didn't know her address, but Beth didn't need to know that.

"Also, this kid's going to have the best auntie ever, so it'll be fine."

"I assume you're referring to yourself and not my sister." Beth rolled her eyes.

"Ah, how is Rachael these days? Still a liability?" Beth was the "good child" to put it politely.

"I haven't spoken to her in a few months. She's gone on another bender with some random guy she met on Bumble."

"Funny you should say that; I downloaded the app the other day."

"You did?"

I'd almost forgotten about Brooke for a split second. Almost.

I shrugged. "Erm . . ."

I'd be lying if I said I hadn't thought about her an unhealthy amount since stepping off the plane. I scanned the airport crowd and the cars we passed on the expressway wondering if she was close by.

Was that normal? I wasn't sure anymore.

My fear in coming to Tokyo was I might take ten steps back. My mind would be consumed with thoughts of her again, not that the thoughts ever went away, but in recent months I'd managed to keep them at bay. I feared the walls I'd put up would crumble around me as soon as my feet landed on Japanese soil.

That was *not* what was happening. I had everything under control.

"I feel okay about it. I'm a little anxious, but I'll be fine." The heart palpitations and dizziness disagreed.

"What makes you anxious?" Beth curled her knees up, ready for a real conversation.

"I guess, knowing she's here somewhere. I'm finally in the same time zone as her. Six thousand miles has now reduced to what, maybe one hundred? If she's still where she moved originally. Sometimes, I wish I could erase it all. I don't want to think about her as much as I do."

Erasing all memory of Brooke would've allowed me to move on with my life, but if that were an option, would I take it? Or did the memory of my time with Brooke outweigh the heartbreak?

"Is that why you've been putting off taking this trip?" Beth asked.

"Partly."

"What's the other part?" Beth reached for the bottle of wine and topped up our half-empty glasses.

"It's maybe not so much now, but last year I couldn't shake this feeling. What if she came back and I wasn't there? What if she changed her mind? I thought she'd come back. For a long time I hoped she'd come storming through my office door and tell me she'd made a huge mistake." I smiled softly, trying hard not to let the emotion result in tears. I'd done enough crying over Brooke Jacobs.

"She'd tell me all she'd found in Japan was heartbreak, and her life wasn't the same without me. I dreamt about it for a long time. Then the weeks turned into months, and I realised she wasn't coming back. It sounds ridiculous when I say it out loud."

Beth reached for my arm. "It's not, Holly."

"I'm pining after a girl who didn't want me. She quite happily gave up a life with me for what? To sit at the top of her dad's tower locked away like a damsel in distress, until her father finds her a suitable boyfriend?" There was a fury inside my veins whenever I thought of him.

Beth smirked. "Are you describing Rapunzel?"

I picked up the small decorative cushion and threw it at her, narrowly missing the glass of wine delicately balanced between her fingertips. "Stop it! And this is why I never tell you anything, but yes, it does sound very Rapunzel-esque." I laughed.

"You literally tell me everything."

"How do you know?" I replied smugly.

"Okay, tell me something important I don't know about?" Beth said confidently.

"Last year I hooked up with a friend of a friend of Paula's, and the next day she wanted to go for breakfast, but I told her I thought I'd made a mistake, and I was in love with someone else."

Beth finished my story. "And when she asked who, you said my name, because it was the first name to come into your head that wasn't Brooke."

"Yes . . . How did you . . . Okay well, I never told you what really happened the night you blacked out on your nineteenth birthday."

"Yes, you did. You kissed my sister."

"Shit. Did I tell you that?" I laughed.

"Yes, you told me a year later because the guilt was eating you up inside." Beth raised her eyebrow. "It was just a kiss, right?"

"Yes, absolutely." Unfortunately, Beth's sister was hot.

"Do you know I had to work from home once because I cried so hard watching a film I was emotionally distraught for days after?"

"Yes, when Mufasa died in *The Lion King*. You called me the next day and asked me to send help because your tear ducts had dried up, and you thought you might go blind because you couldn't produce any lubricant for your eyes." Beth was smug. She had the memory of a dolphin.

"Oh, now you say it like that, it sounds ridiculous, but I don't think that film is appropriate anymore. It should be rewritten so Mufasa lives and the other one is wiped from existence. It's not fair; it made me emotionally unstable."

I'll never watch it again.

"Do you want to give in yet?" Beth said smugly.

"Did I tell you I slept with the flight attendant on the way over?"

"You're such a liar." Beth chuckled.

"How do you know?"

"This isn't some porno; nobody sleeps with the flight attendant. I think it's frowned upon and not one of the perks of your first-class upgrade."

"Urgh, fine, you win."

"Yes." She punched the air and then reached over and squeezed my hand. "On a serious note, I don't think Brooke quite happily did anything. I think it was hard on her too, but I'm sure she had her reasons. I think she was stupid to let you go, but we all have different levels of courage and different surrounding circumstances."

"It sounds like you're defending her. What's happened to my best friend?"

There was a time when I'd had to ask Beth to stop sending anecdotes about Brooke. I was upset after she left. Beth was angry. Our views on the situation were quite contrasting.

"Absolutely not. I still think her decision was poor, but I feel sorry for her. She'll regret it one day if she doesn't already."

"Maybe, or maybe she's living her happily ever after with some guy named Hiroshi who drives a bright blue Lexus and wears a watch equivalent to my yearly salary."

"You've really thought that through. I like the name Hiroshi. I might suggest it to Ren." She typed a note in her phone as fast as her fingers would allow.

"Glad I could be of service." I looked at my lap. There were crumbs everywhere. "I'm sorry. I'm making such a mess." I scraped at the crumbs until they landed in my hand, and I tossed them back in the empty packet.

My eyes felt heavy. "I think it's time for bed."

"How about you lie down here." Beth patted at the pillow on her lap. "I'll soothingly massage your head until you fall asleep, like old times."

The yawns started. "You're the best."
"I know."

CHAPTER FOUR

Half-conscious I heard my phone vibrating.

I slapped at the bedside table, searching for the source of noise so I could stop the incessant buzzing. When my hands didn't find my phone, I launched upwards only to realise I wasn't at home. My phone was across the room on the desk.

What time is it?

It was dark, and I had no idea how I even ended up in bed. I threw back the covers and stomped over to my phone; it was Paula.

"Yes." I raced back to bed and buried my half naked body within the sheets. Beth had undressed me too? It was just like old times.

"Good evening, sunshine," Paula said all chirpy.

I pulled my phone from my ear to witness the time. "Paula, it's 4 a.m."

"Oh, right. Totally forgot about the time difference. Whoops. Well, whilst I've got you." I sighed, furiously pulling the covers above my head. My eyes hadn't adjusted to even the small light coming from the monitor in the corner.

"If this is about work, I will kill you," I said. She could've at least given me twenty-four hours before breaking the no work talk on vacation code.

"Oh no, not yet, but I do have some gossip for you." I could practically hear the desperation in her voice. She was terrible at keeping secrets.

"The gossip can't wait until a reasonable hour?" I mumbled.

"Nope."

"Okay." I sighed. "Hit me with it."

"Guess who's pregnant?"

I didn't like guessing games. Paula loved to make me guess. She wouldn't know about Beth. She barely even knew Beth. They'd met three times, briefly, so that was out of the question.

"I have no idea." I was too tired to care.

"Are you sat down?"

"I'm lying down because it's 4 a.m. and I'm in bed."

"Snarky."

"Paula, please tell me."

She took two large breaths. The suspense was too dramatised. This better be good.

"Danielle is pregnant." The line went silent.

My eyes shot open, and I jolted upright.

"Danielle, as in the woman I spent eight years of my life with. That Danielle?"

"No, Danielle who works behind the bar at my local pub. Of course that Danielle." Paula scoffed.

"What? How?"

"Well, this thing happens when a man and a woman—"

I interrupted, "Very funny. I can't believe it. Who told you?" I was alert, and it no longer felt like the middle of the night.

"Ashleigh from work has a cousin who is best friends with a girl called Emma. This Emma girl has a brother called Ryan. He told Emma he'd been approached to be a sperm donor for two girls named Danielle and Sophie." Paula reeled off any story like she was reading from a newspaper article. She was articulate and fact driven.

"Seriously?" I shrieked. "They've been together a year. She barely knows the girl."

"You lesbians move fast," Paula pointed out. It was true; we were an act now think later kind of community. I had no deep feelings about the situation. I left that relationship for a reason. She wanted kids and marriage in her future, and I didn't, at least not with her.

The door creaked open. Beth stood in a set of pineapple pyjamas with her matching eye mask shoved up into her hair.

She rubbed at her eyes. "What's going on? I heard yelling."

She closed the door behind her and sauntered over to the bed. "Move over."

"Paula's just telling me Danielle is pregnant." I wiggled my eyebrows.

"The Danielle?"

"Yep."

"Damn, she moves fast."

"Exactly what I said." I placed the phone on loudspeaker so she could be part of the conversation. Paula gave us a five-minute rundown of everything she'd heard from Ashleigh, every detail down to the clothes Ashleigh was wearing, which held absolutely no relevance.

"Wait, what did you say then?" I asked.

"I said Ashleigh told me in confidence, so please don't say anything," Paula replied.

"No, you said something about Francesca."

"Oh, I said Ashleigh told me outside the building at work, before she went for lunch with Francesca."

I found that strange.

"Since when have Ashleigh and Francesca been friends?" I asked.

"They met at your birthday party last year. Don't you remember? They really hit it off. Since then, they've been close friends."

"How did I not know that?" I needed to start paying more attention to the world around me.

"You're always preoccupied at work. I assumed you knew."

I didn't know how I felt about it, but there was a burning in my chest. Was it jealousy? Beth leaned her head against my shoulder.

"Are they dating? I thought Ashleigh was straight?"

"She is straight; they're just good friends as far as I'm aware." Paula paused. "I like Francesca. You should try and rekindle things with her."

If only it was that easy. I'd been tempted ever since my birthday. The truth was, I liked her too, but I couldn't create the space she deserved in my head or my heart, at least not yet.

"You've said this to me at least once a month since my thirtieth birthday party."

"That's because you're an idiot, and I like to remind you how foolish you can be sometimes. There's a gorgeous Italian woman with no baggage, a banging body, and an accent that could make me turn gay, and you are pining after a stuck-up daddy's girl with serious identity issues."

Silence.

Beth gasped.

"Harsh, Paula," I replied.

"It's true," Paula said. "I'm not saying Brooke couldn't change my opinion, but I like Francesca a lot, and I think she could be good for you."

Paula wasn't the only one; Beth nodded in agreement. I thought Francesca would be good for me too. I didn't deny that. Kale was good for me, but that didn't mean I wanted to have it with every meal because unless it's seasoned it tastes like crap. It was a bad analogy, comparing Francesca to a vegetable, but there had to be something more than the initial attraction. I was trying to be considerate of her feelings.

"This has been a lot for me to digest at 4 a.m. I've woken Beth up. She will punish me for that tomorrow." Beth nodded again. "When I get back to sleep, I'm going to have some weird dream about Danielle and Francesca having a child together. It'll come out looking like me. That's going to ruin my whole day."

"Very specific." Paula chuckled.

"I'll speak to you tomorrow, okay?"

"Sure, sleep well girls. Goodnight."

Beth joined in with a joint goodnight.

I launched the phone into the cushions on the floor and shuffled down into a more comfortable position. Beth snuggled in beside me. The pineapple themed eye mask had already been lowered.

"Can we go to sleep now?" she muttered.

"Sure, sorry for waking you."

*

The intention to sleep was there, but it never transpired. When Beth began to stir at 7:30 a.m. I'd been awake for three hours digesting the information. The easy part was being happy for Danielle, we didn't speak anymore, her choice not mine, but I understood her reasoning. All I wanted was the best for her.

After careful self-reflection in the months after Brooke left, I realised I'd perceived my relationship with Danielle inaccurately. In my mind, I'd fought for what we had. I tried to make her happy despite my feelings changing over time, but all I'd done was communicate poorly and continue to do whatever made me happy, whether Danielle agreed or not. In short, I was a bit of an ass. It wasn't always like that, at least I didn't think it was. We were happy at one time, but I lost my way and became quite selfish in my approach.

Point being, the self-reflection helped.

I sent Danielle a letter apologising for the way I handled the end of our relationship. My lack of compassion was cruel. I'd been so focused on my own emotions and the feelings I felt for someone else. I thought "doing the right thing" was ending my relationship with Danielle and moving on quick and sharp. I even told myself it was to "save her pain", but that wasn't true. In reality I was selfish. I was inconsiderate, and I wished wholeheartedly I could go back and do it over again. Danielle never responded to my letter, but she told her mum to tell my mum she appreciated me reaching out—that was enough.

A small part of me was jealous. She'd fallen in love with someone new, someone who wanted the things she did, a family and marriage, and here I was snuggled up to my snoring best friend in a two-bed apartment in Tokyo with absolutely no grip on my life. My job was the only consistent thing I had, and that could all go away with one wrong move, or one violation of bar association rules. One misjudgement resulting in moral turpitude could get me disbarred. Then my professional future as well as my romantic future would go up in flames. I tried not to dwell on that too much.

Then there was Francesca: beautiful, graceful, sweet Francesca. Morally I was doing the right thing by not calling her. I was avoiding a complicated entanglement while hoping and praying my feelings for Brooke would change, allowing me to pursue something deeper and more meaningful with Francesca. The woman walked around London like she'd stepped directly off the catwalk. I knew she got hit on daily, probably five times a day, and one of these days she was going to accept an invitation. And twelve months later, she too would be married with children, and I'd still be all alone.

I didn't like that thought.

"I am doing the right thing, aren't I?" Beth's head flopped to the side as I jumped out of bed and began to pace.

"Huh?"

"By not talking to Francesca, by leaving her alone and dooming myself to an eternity of what ifs. I'm doing the right thing, right?" Saying it out loud didn't convince me of anything. I sounded stupid. As a Lawyer who relies on very specific analytical skills and a sharp attention to detail that wasn't great. "Am I an idiot?"

Beth rubbed at her eyes, yawned, and kicked her legs out from under the covers. "You mean, for not immediately marrying the hot Italian? Probably."

I slumped into the cushions I'd tossed into a pile on the floor the night before. Beth sat staring at me in disbelief as I had a meltdown.

"I'm going to text her."

"Absolutely not." Beth jumped from her position and ripped the phone from my hand at lightning speed. I hated that she could do that, she'd always been so agile and nimble.

"What the hell?"

"You're not texting Francesca. Anything you say whilst you're in this weird mood is dangerous."

"Beth, give me my phone back." The next two minutes resembled our university sorority style pillow fights, except there were never any actual pillows involved, or sororities; it was just a fight for who got the last slice of pizza, and she always won.

"Holly—stop acting like a crazy person!" She scrambled free and launched herself onto the bed to safety. "Hear me out. Okay?"

"Fine." I rubbed at my arm; the red mark was already glowing. She was freakishly strong.

"I think you need to take the next two weeks to think about what you want. Don't make decisions based on a 4 a.m. phone call from Paula, who, let's be honest, is a blabber mouth and adds extra drama into every story."

It was true. I loved Paula, but she was a blabber mouth. Just last year she was told in the strictest confidence that Jason, one of the other paralegals was dating Mr. West's daughter. The next day everyone in the office knew. Apparently, Mr. West didn't even have a daughter, and Jason was having an affair with Mellissa from two floors down; his wife who worked on the same floor wasn't too pleased when she found out.

"What if it's too late? What if I've spent the last twelve months avoiding the love of my life?" It was a long shot. I've read enough books and watched enough movies to know when you know you know.

"Does she feel like the love of your life?" Beth asked.

I shook my head.

"Well then, another couple of weeks won't hurt."

"I hate that you're always right." I smack my hands into the pillows like a child.

"You see this phone? I'm confiscating it." She tucked it into the waistband of her pyjamas.

"You are joking, right? I'm not a child," I said whilst sulking—like a child.

"I don't care. It stays with me until you can be trusted to use it appropriately."

I could jump on the bed and wrestle her for it, but she was pregnant, and she'd still tangle her body in a way that would make MMA fighters recoil, and then beat my ass as always.

"Fine," I admitted defeat.

"Glad we cleared that up. Let's get some breakfast and figure out what we're doing with our day, shall we?"

Beth skipped off towards the kitchen.

I followed.

It was time to plan an itinerary. Distractions were exactly what I needed.

CHAPTER FIVE

We drove from Beth's apartment in Hatagaya to a place called Asakusa; the journey was only twenty-five minutes. Asakusa was known for being the spiritual heart of Tokyo. Our first stop was Sensō-ji Temple. Picture big red pillars, giant lanterns, and a bustling crowd of tourists. We didn't stay in the vicinity for long; the crowds were overwhelming.

Instead, we took a trip through the neighbourhood of Ueno. Beth dragged me down a shopping street called Nakamise.

"I promise they do the best traditional Japanese sweets down here."

It was enough to convince me to follow her anywhere. My sweet tooth often overpowered everything else.

She did make me trapse through every clothing store within the vicinity and any establishment that sold souvenirs from old Japan. We got some freshly baked rice crackers and a handful of Ningyo-yaki.

"You will regret it until the day you die if you don't try these," Beth assured me whilst shoving a small doll-shaped baked cake into my mouth. She was right, as always; they were delicious.

The area was beautiful and historic. It had a friendliness about it; everyone wanted to share their culture and created an atmosphere that made me want to stay and spend my money—which I did, in heaps.

"Do you like this?" Beth presented me with a traditional golden kimono. The lady who ran the store advised Beth that they were all handwoven and of the highest quality. Beth, like me, was a sucker for a good pitch.

"It's really nice." I reached out and ran the silk through my fingers. "Good quality too." I had no idea what a bad quality kimono would look like, if it was even real silk, or handmade, but it would suit Beth; that much I did know.

"I might get it." She grabbed another from the rack, but the black version. "Shall we get matching?"

"Erm . . ."

"We'll take these two please." At least I think that's what she said. She said it in fluent Japanese, and the lady looked stunned, as most locals did when they realised Beth wasn't the predictable tourist.

I guess I'm wearing a kimono tonight.

We arrived in Shibuya next. It wasn't the first time I'd visited the famous Shibuya Crossing. With thousands of pedestrians crossing at once it's known for being one of the most iconic sights in Tokyo. I ticked it off my bucket list on my first trip to Japan. I'd seen it in numerous films, most notably *The Fast and the Furious: Tokyo Drift*. It was surprisingly one of my favourites in the franchise despite not including Paul or Vin.

Experiencing the Shibuya Crossing on the ground didn't give the full effect.

"Shall we head for a coffee?" Beth asked.

"Yes, absolutely."

We found seats inside the Starbucks located in the Tsutaya bookstore. It was a beautiful upscale space with the perfect aerial view of the crossing. We ate a quick young couple vacate the sofa on the eastern side, we made a beeline for it.

We got comfortable and spent the next thirty minutes watching, admiring, and living in the moment. We didn't say a great deal; sometimes it was better that way.

"I could stay up here forever." I sighed.

"Me too."

"I think I'd like to come back here again before I leave," I said.

"We can do that." Beth smiled.

My stomach made a loud grumble. The woman next to us looked my way—totally embarrassing.

"I think I'm hungry."

"Shall we head back to the deck below? The guy said there was a small restaurant."

"Sure, let's do that."

We took the stairs this time; after the galactic elevator I half expected a slide to extend from the side of the building and that be the only way down. Thankfully, it wasn't.

Walking down the steps was surreal. I felt unstable in the vast open space. We were so high up in the Japanese skyline that my legs felt weak, and there was no other preferably more enclosed way down to the lower observation deck. I tried not to look beyond the edge. I concentrated on my feet; taking one step at a time. I wasn't afraid of heights, but the altitude and lack of food in my stomach made me queasy.

I didn't alert Beth. Instead, I focused on the people around me. There was an escalator to the right of the stairs. It headed up in the opposite direction, which did not help the ever-growing feeling I was floating in space.

Wait—

I did a double take.

The escalator was filled with Japanese teens dressed extravagantly in bright colours and platform shoes, but that wasn't what caught my eye. Behind the tall guy with the purple hair and black beret I saw the profile of a woman with bouncy blonde hair.

Surely that's not—it couldn't be.

I stopped immediately.

The moment was like something out of a movie. I left Beth stomping down the steep steps and ran back up, one step after another, but the escalator was moving too fast. I tried to run, but the crowds charged towards me with purpose. I was the inconvenience shoving past people to get a better look at *her*.

It was impossible.

She was gone. I refrained from shouting. I only saw the back of her head as the person beside her whispered in her ear.

No, my mind was playing tricks on me. I had a feeling that would happen.

"Hol, what are you doing?" Realising I'd gone AWOL, Beth clambered after me. "Holly, hold on. What's wrong?"

It couldn't have been her.

Could it?

The odds were slim at best.

I shook my head. "Sorry, I thought . . . Never mind."

"You looked possessed. Don't scare me like that." She whacked my arm, and we continued down the stairs. I turned towards the elevator once, twice, and a final time—nothing.

Whoever it was, she was gone.

*

The observation deck was something to behold. We sat on a sofa with 360-degree views of the city. Unfortunately, we were limited to fifty minutes due to high demand.

"Who can eat in fifty minutes?" I said to Beth.

It turned out the food menu consisted of bar snacks, so it didn't matter because mixed nuts would have to see me through until dinner. My heart rate wouldn't settle, even the hair on my head felt heavy. I was beginning to sweat; the heat was taking its toll on my exhausted body. I needed a distraction.

"How high up do you think we are?" I said.

"Weren't you paying attention? It said 230 metres on the sign over there." Beth didn't seem phased we were basically on the same level as an aeroplane.

"I don't feel like that sounds high. What does 230 metres equate too? Maybe like ninety-seven giraffes?" I shrugged.

"That is specific, and it's hard to scale using giraffes as your measurement." Beth laughed.

"True. How about three football pitches?"

She looked towards the skyline, deep in thought.

"A regulation tennis court is around twenty-three metres, so it's basically ten tennis courts."

She was smart. "Huh, I expected more."

I wanted to order the champagne drinks package, but I remembered the reason to celebrate was also the reason it wasn't appropriate to drink champagne, so I settled for a mocktail in solidarity with Beth.

"We should have come here at night. I bet the skyline is incredible." The feel of the plush grey padding on the chair cushioned my back perfectly.

"We can come back. We might need to book though. I'm told it's even busier in the evenings," Beth said.

The view should've been the only thing occupying my mind. Instead, my eyes wandered from one corner of the deck to the next, searching for the girl with blonde hair.

I needed to be certain it wasn't *her*.

"What are you looking for?" Beth asked.

"Erm . . . Tokyo Tower." I pointed towards the tall red tower in the distance—quick thinking. "I don't get it though, why is it a landmark? It just looks like they plonked Blackpool tower in the middle of Tokyo."

"Are you seriously comparing Blackpool tower to the famous Tokyo Tower? For starters it's twice the size."

"Is it?" I shrugged. I'd only seen Blackpool tower once on a school trip. I remember it towering above everything else, and to a teenager with stunted growth it seemed huge.

"You're on edge," Beth pointed out.

I didn't look at her. She could read me like a book. I avoided eye contact, but I could feel hers burning into my peripheral vision.

"I'm fine," I replied, unconvincingly.

A light bulb moment spread across her face; her eyebrows arched; her lips cracked open. She knew.

"You thought you saw Brooke, didn't you?"

How did she—

It was pointless to lie, so I nodded.

"For a split second."

I half expected to be ridiculed, but she did something I didn't think she would. She reached over and grasped my hand; her smile was sympathetic.

"I think the chances of her being up here at the same time as us are pretty slim, so don't worry. It won't have been her." She shook her head, confident in her answer.

It was a logical response.

I'd never felt so much disappointment mixed with relief; it was a bizarre combination.

"I know. I think my heart stopped." I lifted her hand up and pressed it against my chest. "Feel it now; it's still beating like crazy. Imagine what it would be like if I saw her." I sipped on my mai tai mocktail, which was better than the real thing. Nobody actually liked the taste of alcohol, right? I certainly didn't; I just liked the way it made me feel—sometimes—in that moment I needed a stronger drink. I awaited Beth's wisdom.

"It would be quite the spectacle."

"The thought scares me to death. What would I say?" I was speaking hypothetically. That was all I had. It would never happen, but that hadn't stopped me fantasising about what I would say for the past two years.

"You just say, hello? How've you been? How's Japan? Hey, I don't suppose your dad has stopped being a massive homophobic asshole yet?" Beth smirked. "See how easy that was? I can think of countless things."

"Don't . . ." I sighed.

"Seriously, if it happens, just be yourself." I rolled my eyes. It would be impossible to be myself in that situation. I remembered having a crush on my mum's best friend's daughter in college. I thought it was cool to lean casually against the fish tank on the dining table whilst I lifted my top ever so slightly and told her all about my teenage abs and how I wanted to be a professional athlete. I absolutely did not, but I'd overheard her say she thought abs were sexy. I also didn't have abs, but if I creased my stomach hard enough I could more or less create some. Anyway, my idiocy came back to bite me in the ass when I slipped, and my hand went into the tank.

In hindsight I was glad. I'd been one step away from putting on an Elvis Presley accent and saying something stupid like, *How ya doing, little lady?*

Beth nudged my arm. "Maybe you could tell her you've got a hot girlfriend called Francesca... And you're engaged and about to move to... what's that place called? The one with the pastel-coloured houses on the hill?"

"Positano?"

"That's the one. You're going to move to Positano and live happily ever after, spending night after night falling in love and falling out of champagne bars with a stomach full of pasta."

"You paint quite the picture."

She spied the glass of champagne on the next table and proceeded to sip her mocktail. "I hate pregnancy already," she muttered under her breath.

I'd considered it. Recently, I'd been thinking more about Francesca, and how she could've been everything I needed. "It sounds nice, doesn't it? The Italian lifestyle."

"It could be your lifestyle." She raised her eyebrows suggestively.

"Except it's not and probably never will be. I think I royally screwed up that one."

I'm an idiot.

"Even if you did. Brooke doesn't need to know." Beth wiggled her eyebrows.

"I can't say any of that because it's a lie. Besides, you're talking like I'm going to see her." I could feel the heat rising in my chest.

"Stop being such a lawyer. You're not under oath now. It's good to lie. You don't want her to think you're moping around, do you?"

"Again, it's irrelevant, but is that what I'm doing? Moping?" I sulked.

"Just a smidge, but I get it."

Beth pulled at the small curly strands of hair she'd left dangling down beside her ears. She had no makeup on, and she looked radiant. It was enviable.

"Can I just say, if Ren left me, I would make damn sure I told a million lies until he was so distraught with jealousy that he came crawling right back. I'd be dating the Japanese equivalent of Mr. Grey. I'd be dating some heir to the throne who had nothing better to do than spend all his millions on me. I'd pretend I had a beautifully sculpted stripper turned businessman who liked to grind on me all day, spin me around, and rub his sexy oiled eight-pack against my body whilst I watched him play with power tools butt naked."

"Erm . . . okay. Kind of feels like you described *Magic Mike*."

"I did, yes. Channing Tatum is every girl's dream— Well, every *straight* girl's dream," she corrected herself.

"I can see the appeal." I chuckled.

The next forty minutes flew by. I finished my mocktail and with Beth's blessing switched to the hard stuff. I told myself a brandy would take the edge off, but it was going to take more than a drink to get Brooke off my mind while we were both in Japan.

*

The elevator ride down to the fourteenth floor coupled with the strobe lighting sent my stomach into a frenzy; I felt as though I'd been on a fairground ride. We collected our belongings and made our way to the exit. My shoulder bore the weight of my purchases once again.

A hand grabbed my shoulder as I manoeuvred my way through the crowds of people.

"Excuse me." I didn't recognise the voice.

I spun around so quickly I stumbled sideways into a large expensive looking potted plant. Luckily, it was so expensive it was heavy enough to stay rooted to the ground as I bent the branches almost to a snapping point.

"Woah, sorry."

The young man grabbed my hand and helped me up. Beth half helped with her free hand but was too busy laughing at my almost becoming a human shaped gardenia.

"I didn't mean to startle you." He held up his hand apologetically. He had a black apron on and a name badge written in Japanese. He must've been staff.

"It's okay. Can I help you?"

"I was asked to deliver a message from a young woman over by the elevator." He pointed towards the area I'd just vacated. My eyes shot left to right. People were queuing, but there was nobody I recognised.

"Wait . . . What? Who? What did she look like?"

"She had blonde hair, a little bit shorter than you." He gestured to his shoulder for a height gauge.

"She was English," he added.

I steadied myself. Beth stopped laughing.

"She didn't give me her name, but she said to tell you she'll be at Chaos Kitchen tomorrow at 7 p.m." He smiled proudly. He'd delivered his message, but he'd had no idea how powerful that message was going to be.

"Where's Chaos Kitchen?" I asked. My head jolting back and forth on a swivel. I wanted to scream, *Someone tell me where Chaos Kitchen is immediately*, but I remained calm—

"It's in the basement of Shibuya Parco," he said triumphantly.

"Where is Shibuya Parco?" He turned to leave, his job done, but it wasn't enough. What else did she say? How did she sound? What was she wearing? Was she smiling? Did she smell nice? Who was she with?

"It's about five minutes that way." He pointed to the right. Before I had a chance to ask anything else he was backpedalling. "I've gotta run. Take care."

The young man with spiky black hair reached for his headphones and placed them neatly back in his ears.

"Holy shit," Beth cursed.

I was right.

It was Brooke.

CHAPTER SIX

The clock on the wall stopped—it literally stopped. That's how long I'd been staring at it; even the clock had given up. If I paced back and forth across Beth's kitchen any longer, there would be a size five shaped Converse imprint on the floor.

The weather outside had been beautiful all day, reaching temperatures of twenty-eight degrees. According to the tour guide who I'd made friends with over Facebook, today made for a perfect day to climb Mount Fuji, but my mind was too preoccupied to set off on a potentially hazardous climbing trip. Even with the weather on my side, it was still unpredictable terrain.

I hated myself for being two days into my trip and allowing the thoughts of Brooke to consume me. I'd barely slept the night before; the thought of being in the same vicinity as her sent shivers down my spine. I'd been so close; I could've touched her. My arm could've brushed past hers in and amongst the tourist chaos, and I wouldn't have known.

Had she been watching me?
When did she notice I was there?
Why didn't she come and speak to me?
Why the messenger?

The questions had played on my mind all night, and before I knew it the first appearance of sunlight coloured the horizon. I was exhausted.

Beth drove us to Ueno Park at lunchtime. It was one of Tokyo's largest public parks. It was a distraction, but

I couldn't shake her. We'd ventured inside Tokyo's National Museum and cast our eyes upon the famous Shinobazu Pond, which during the summer months was covered in pink lotus flowers. Coupled with the hundreds of blossom trees, it was an aesthetically pleasing experience. The scenery made for a few nice Instagram worthy photos. I sent a quick snap to Paula. She replied with a middle finger emoji, followed by heart eyes. Typical.

We arrived back at Beth's apartment four hours later, and the panic set in. My fingers began to tingle. My stomach churned, and I felt absent from my body.

"What do I do?" I asked Beth.

"We've gone over this, Hol." She was sprawled across the sofa with her feet up against the wall and her hips elevated by the countless scatter cushions. It was the same relaxed lounging position she favoured at university. The kind of position you take if you're trying to fall pregnant, except she'd already done that.

"I know. But she said, 'I'll be at Chaos Kitchen at seven'. What does that even mean?"

I reached into the freezer for an ice pack to cool my body, which currently felt like the bonnet of a black car in the height of summer.

"Is that an invitation? Is it just a statement? Is she letting me know that's where she'll be so I can avoid it? Does she want to see me? Why get some random guy to tell me that? Why didn't she come and speak to me herself?"

I ran the ice pack across my forehead, down my arms, and onto my chest; it was freezing cold, but the shock helped me focus.

"You'll have to ask her all those things when you see her," Beth huffed.

She half-rolled back out of her position and marched over to the kitchen island. She pulled the chair out from underneath the breakfast bar and gestured for me to sit. I did as I was told.

"Turn around." I spun to sit with my back to her, and she softly released my hair from my high ponytail. I had it off my neck for a reason, but I refrained from commenting. I liked it when Beth played with my hair; it calmed me. She gently tugged at the ends with her fingers to loosen any knots.

"I shouldn't see her, should I? It's written all over your face." I sighed.

"Holly, nothing I say is going to change your mind. You know you're going to see her. From there you can make up your mind, but . . ."

I let my head roll back to look at Beth, but she pushed it forwards and continued to tend to my hair. It felt like she was plaiting it, which was something we used to do throughout university. Whenever either one of us felt stressed or anxious, we would plait each other's hair. It was still just as relaxing.

"But what?" I asked.

"Ask yourself why? Why are you going to go? What are your expectations? You need to be careful with those."

"I don't have expectations."

"Do you know why?" Her voice was calm and soothing.

"Ow." My head jerked backwards.

"Sorry, your hair was tangled." She chuckled.

What was my why? It was a good question. It's not like we could be together. She lived on the other side of the world. She had a whole new life, and our time had been and gone, right? As much as the thought pained me, I had to be realistic.

"When she asked me to meet her at Nina's Café a few years ago I thought I'd be gaining some clarity. I felt like I'd made progress since we ended things, and meeting up would be the final step in the moving on process. Does that make sense?"

I could see Beth's head nodding in the reflection on the fridge.

"But I felt ambushed when she told me about her move to Japan. It threw me completely."

"I remember you calling. It was hard to see you like that," Beth said.

"That's when she gave me the letter. I thought reading it would give me the clarity I needed."

"It didn't?" Beth asked.

"No, the letter became my obsession. It was the last piece of her. It was the only thing I had of her which nobody could take from me, and I've held on to it these past couple of years like it's the most precious thing in the world." I gulped.

It was hard to admit.

Beth reached around and brushed my hair behind my ears. I tried not to get upset.

"She told me to promise I would keep the letter forever, and I took that literally. I'm afraid if I don't see her again, I won't get the closure I'm desperately seeking. I want to understand. Until I do, I'm afraid I'll never be free from this tightening in my chest. It reminds me every single day that she was real."

"Turn around," she whispered.

I swivelled, almost knocking the glass off the counter as I steadied myself. My eyes glazed over, but I was trying desperately not to let the tears fall.

"What is it you have a hard time understanding?" Beth asked softly.

That was easy.

"Why wasn't I enough?"

*

Chaos Kitchen was exactly as the name suggested—chaotic.

The vibrant decor brought it to life. The wide range of restaurants on offer made it extremely difficult to know where Brooke was situated. The smell of food overwhelmed my senses. They had everything on offer from beef ramen, to teppanyaki, and my favourite, deep-fried kushikatsu; the combination of skewered meat and seasoned vegetables was second to none.

The tight alleyway packed with an array of food stands reminded me of the food hall at Camden Market, but it was indoors and more extravagant. Each restaurant had its own unique theme, and the neon signs and reflective decor seemed to be a winning aesthetic.

I roamed the area with no idea where to go. The place was bigger than I'd anticipated. I stumbled upon a corner dedicated to unusual foods; when I saw fried insects on the menu I turned back immediately. I didn't sign up for the Japanese version of *I'm a Celebrity . . . Get Me Out of Here!* I couldn't imagine Brooke would have either; that section of the food court could go safely untouched.

"Please, madam, try?" A middle-aged woman stood at the entrance to a small eatery with high wooden bar stools. She held out a platter filled with gyoza—my favourite.

"We do the best pan-fried dumplings. Please, try one." I obliged even though I was so nervous I felt sick.

"Thank you so much."

She wasn't lying; the taste left my mouth crying out for more. "They're delicious."

"Of course. Would you like to dine with us?" She smiled.

"I'm meeting someone, but I will come back."

"Have a nice day." She nodded. The interaction eased my anxiety.

The place was full of so many dead ends and unexpected angles that I quickly felt disorientated. As I made my way around, I looked in each restaurant and perused the menus one at a time. I made a mental note to return to a place called Izakaya Masaka, mainly due to the smell of fried mushrooms. A customer left with a parting message, "Try the mock karaage in sweet and sour flavour; you'll not be disappointed"—I made a note in my phone.

I felt like I was going in circles. I had no end destination, no sign to look out for, no inkling where Brooke might be. There were five thousand heavily occupied eateries. I rounded another corner; a silver sign that read *Sake Bar* caught my eye.

There were numerous Japanese symbols I didn't understand, so I was grateful for the English translations on most of the signs. I tried to recall what Beth told me about sake. It was an alcoholic beverage, that much I knew. It had something to do with rice and fermenting, the details didn't matter all that much. I liked the aesthetic of the bar, it was dark in decor with a wooden element; the barstools looked comfortable, unlike the harder wooden ones in the other bars. It was busy, which I thought was a good sign. I scanned the menu and decided to take a seat. I figured walking around aimlessly wasn't helping, so sitting on a perch with a decent view of my surroundings made me feel more at ease, and a drink couldn't hurt.

My head was buried deep in the menu when I felt a presence to my left. I didn't look up right away, but I could see their legs and a pair of black Converse in my peripheral vision.

"Hi there. Welcome to Sake Bar, will you be having a drink with us today?" It was an odd thing to say in a bar. What else would I be doing other than having a drink? But it wasn't the words I found the most disconcerting, it was the *voice*.

I would've recognised that voice anywhere. If I was submerged in water one thousand miles away from that bar, I would've recognised that sweet raspy voice. I couldn't look up immediately. My body was stiff. I was frozen in place.

Was this really happening?

I didn't respond; I just turned my head, and as I did Brooke glanced up from her notepad and looked me dead in the eye.

"Oh, hi."

"Hi." I gulped.

She wiped her forehead before subconsciously patting down her apron. She looked as nervous as I felt. She ran her fingertips through the front of her hair, trying to tame the wispy parts; she hated them, but they were my favourite.

I couldn't take my eyes off her lips. They were more rounded than I remembered. Her chocolate brown eyes locked with mine, and the hint of a smile crept across her lips until she dropped her gaze completely.

"You're early. I don't get off for another fifteen minutes."

"You work here?" I asked.

"Yep. Do you want a drink whilst you wait?"
"Sure. I can do that."

Brooke placed an order with the bartender. I tried to compose myself. I watched her move from one table to the next; each time she glanced my way for a brief second.

Was she checking I hadn't left?

A minute later she placed a fancy cocktail glass in front of me; it was white in colour with a lime wedge. I reached into my pocket for some money, but Brooke quickly placed her hand on my arm.

"Don't insult me please; it's on me."

"Thank you." I didn't move my arm, and she didn't remove her hand. The faintest of touches was all it took to catapult me back in time two years.

"What's it called?" I nodded towards the glass.

"White Mountain. I think you'll enjoy it." Brooke smiled. When she removed her hand she brushed her fingertips along the length of my arm, purposefully or not, it was effective.

I waited and watched for the next fifteen minutes as she finished up her shift. A wry familiar smile crept across her face every time she came close to me.

It felt surreal seeing her in person. For the past two years she had been a figment of my imagination, someone I thought I would only ever see again in my dreams. Throughout my adult life I had met a lot of women, most of whom cared too much about their appearance, their nails, or their hair, but not Brooke. She shone so effortlessly without any of that. Her purple nail varnish was chipped. Her hair was mostly scraped back into a messy bun, but her face was blemish free with just a glowing moisturised complexion. She looked exactly like I remembered, and when she smiled my whole body rejoiced.

*

"When you asked me to meet you here, I didn't realise you worked here." I glanced at her as we strolled through the food hall.

"It was supposed to be temporary, but I enjoy it. The people are great, and working with customers has helped me pick up the Japanese language as well." Brooke grinned.

"You can speak Japanese?"

Brooke nodded triumphantly.

That was impressive. It took Beth close to three years to become at ease with the language, and she still struggled with certain phrases and words.

We passed a bar called Campy!bar, where a drag queen with cropped pink hair and eccentric eye makeup waved in our direction.

"*Kon'nichiwa*," The drag queen called out, "*Shifuto wa dōdeshita ka?*"

"*Heikin. Isogashī?*" Brooke replied.

Another drag queen approached. They had a tall ginger Amy Winehouse hairstyle with a large pink flower buried into the bee's nest and costume earrings the size of my hands.

"Mada," the one with the pink hair replied. The whole conversation, bar the opening line, went straight over my head. I knew how to say "Hello", that was the extent of my Japanese. Beth tried to teach me a little every time I came over, but when my feet touched on British ground again I instantly forgot.

"*Anata no tomodachi wa kawaīdesu.*" The one with the ginger hair waved with the tips of their fingers and blew a kiss in my direction. Brooke giggled nervously and waved back. "*Ja nee, redīsu.*"

"Look at you!" My eyes widened. Her accent was impressive; she almost sounded fluent. "I have no idea what you said; please translate."

"Delta, with the pink hair, asked how work was. I said it was average. I asked if she was busy. She replied, 'not yet'. Wanda, with the ginger hair, said, 'you're cute'."

"Oh, cute, huh?" I blushed.

"Can't blame her can you?" Brooke's gaze fell to the floor. She quickly changed the subject. "Are you hungry?"

"Starving," I replied.

"Okay, follow me. I know just the place."

We arrived outside a restaurant without neon lights and bright colours. It had exposed brick on the outside, traditional red tapestry on the inside, and basic wooden tables and chairs. The front looked familiar. When I clocked the name and examined the menu it was Izakaya Masaka—the place I'd written in the notes on my phone.

"I saw this place on the way in." The waiter guided us to a two-seater table in the corner.

"You'll love it. They do the best gyoza in the area, if you ask me. The teriyaki mayonnaise is unreal, and it's entirely plant based."

I spied the food on the table's as we passed through; it looked unbelievable.

"Are you vegetarian?"

She nodded. "I decided to stop eating meat about a year ago."

"Really? How come?"

"I watched a video online . . ." I pulled the stool from underneath the table, gesturing for her to take a seat. She paused. It felt natural for me to be chivalrous with her, but I could see the confusion in her eyes.

"Thank you . . . So, I ended up down a rabbit hole researching the health benefits. When I read I was less likely to develop cancer and heart disease I was sold. Apparently, every vegetarian or vegan saves about two hundred animals a year, and I love animals." She shrugged, as if making such a strong life choice wasn't a big deal.

"I can't imagine it's easy to be vegetarian over here? Doesn't everything involve fish or meat?" It might have been stereotypical of me to assume, but I recalled Beth attempting a vegan diet a few years back and failing miserably.

She gestured towards the vegan menu in front of me.

"You just have to find the right places. It's not as popular as it is in England, but it's becoming more normalised."

She pointed towards a section on the menu. "Kaarage fried chicken is still your favourite Japanese dish, right?"

She remembered.

"Yes . . ."

There was nothing quite like the ultra-crispy chicken with a soy sauce marinade. My mouth watered at the thought of the salty goodness.

"This place does the vegan version, before you turn your nose up, it's unbelievable. Trust me."

She must've noticed the dazed look on my face.

"You look surprised." Brooke paused. "You didn't think I'd remember your favourite foods?" she scoffed.

I smirked. "I didn't expect you to."

"I remember everything about you, Holly." She fiddled with the edges of the laminated menu. "I'd never forget."

The air around us shifted. My hair stood on end. I believed her because I remembered everything about her too. Brook averted her gaze; she broke the tension just as the waiter came to take our orders.

Brooke ordered two lots of the mock kaarage, one with sweet and sour glaze and another with teriyaki mayonnaise, and two lemon sour drinks.

"Lemon sour?" I scrunched my face at the thought.

"It's really nice. The lemon isn't overpowering; don't worry. I know you hate things that are too citrusy." There she goes again.

The loud atmosphere of Chaos Kitchen could be felt through the open doorway. Inside, tucked away in the corner, it felt more intimate. The soft sound of traditional Japanese music peacefully echoed around us.

"It's nice here," I said.

"The music takes you away to a different place if you let it. Shut your eyes," Brooke instructed. I thought she was joking at first. "Just do it. Trust me."

I did. I'd do anything she asked. Still.

"Now, picture cherry blossom trees swaying in the wind and a large pond filled with fish. They're rising to the surface every so often to create a silent ripple, but you can hear the *plop* as they sink back under."

"Plop? Really?" I opened my left eye, my right remained squeezed shut.

She laughed. "I don't know what other word to use to describe it; it sounds like a plop."

Brooke reached over the table and used her hand to brush my eyes shut. "There's a bamboo basket filled with delicious freshly picked fruit . . . and . . . Yeah, that's all I've got."

I opened my eyes.

"That sounds a bit like Ueno Park. Me and Beth went there today."

"It's beautiful, isn't it? I go there sometimes to read; it's what I imagine when people say the essence of Japan." Brooke smiled politely as the waiter placed our bright yellow drinks on the table.

"*Arigatō*," She thanked him.

"So . . ." There was so much I wanted to say, but I wanted to keep it light-hearted. "Who was that random guy you asked to deliver a message?" That part I was curious about.

"Just a random guy." She shrugged. "I thought it was you. I couldn't be 100 percent sure, but I saw your profile and well . . ."

"Well, what?"

"I don't see women like you that often." She took a sip of her drink; her lips pursed, which told me I was right, and it was sour.

"Women like me? Should I be offended?" I laughed.

"No, of course not." She shook her head. "You're just so strong-jawed and sharp. You look like you mean business in a compelling sort of way; it's unusual. I'm going to stop talking now." She fidgeted with her nails instead, picking at the remaining nail varnish.

"Thank you, I guess." I laughed. "Why didn't you come and talk to me yourself?"

"Nerves, mainly, but I was with . . . my brother." She hesitated. That's who was whispering in her ear. I took satisfaction in knowing it wasn't a boyfriend.

"How is Tom?" I asked through gritted teeth.

"You don't care, do you?" Brooke said.

"Nope. I'm being polite."

Tom was the product of his father, a prick, for the want of a better word. I knew exactly how he was getting on from my occasional stalking of Instagram, but she didn't need to know that.

"I don't want to talk about my brother."

Good, me neither, I thought.

Brooke started tapping her fingers on the table. Then, for the first time since we'd sat down, she made real eye contact with me, and she didn't look away until the waiter arrived with our food.

"How long are you here?" Brooke asked.

"Two weeks."

"When did you fly in?"

"Two days ago," I said. What looked like relief washed over her face. What did that mean?

"If I said I'd like to show you somewhere tomorrow, would you say yes?"

I nodded. "Sure, I'd just have to check with Beth."

"Okay."

I tried the mock karaage with sweet and sour dressing—delicious. I didn't feel hungry when it arrived. I was desperately trying to control my griping stomach. I felt sick with anticipation, but I ate it regardless.

"What do you think?" Brooke asked.

"Unbelievable."

"As good as chicken?"

"I'm not sure about that, but damn close."

Brooke picked up a small piece of her teriyaki flavoured karaage and leaned across the table. "Try this."

I opened my mouth around the chopsticks, trying as neatly as possible to remove the food without coming across as sensual in any way.

"Mmm . . . Wow, that one's better."

The lemon sour alcohol came with free refills, which said a lot really. It wasn't a drink I would choose again, but my palate became numb to the sourness after a while. The restaurant soon began closing the kitchen. That was our cue to leave.

I followed Brooke's lead as we strolled back towards the escalators. I didn't want the night to end. Our bodies brushed together as I held the door open for her to exit onto the busy streets of Shibuya.

"Do you know how to get back to Beth's?" Brooke asked.

"I texted her. She's going to pick me up." I wanted to say, *When I'm ready*, but I got the impression Brooke had other places to be.

"Good."

Brooke stepped closer with confidence; she held out her hand. "Your phone." I reached into my back pocket. I'd remembered to get it back from Beth after the whole confiscating incident. Brooke created a new contact and typed in her number with the Japanese dialling code.

"Text me when you're home safe, and I'll see you tomorrow?" It was more of a question than a statement. Did she want reassurance?

"Sure, I'll look forward to it."

She balanced on her tiptoes to wrap her arms around my neck. I placed one hand on the base of her back; the other held my phone by my side. She pressed her mouth into the dip between my shoulder and my collarbone before she pulled away.

"Bye."

"Hey, Brooke . . ." I called. She turned back. "Don't you think it's crazy we bumped into each other yesterday? Japan's a big country. What are the odds?"

"Not really. I believe when you think about someone or something a lot, the universe has a way of making it happen."

She pulled at her zip hoodie, wrapping it around her body.

"See you tomorrow, Holly."

CHAPTER SEVEN

The next day Ren arrived home early from his work trip, and Beth informed me they had a lot of "house things" to take care of—whatever that meant. I was grateful she wanted to get rid of me. It made me feel less guilty about wanting to spend more time with Brooke. Although, had Brooke not been in the picture, I know Beth would've postponed any menial chores she had to do to spend time with me.

The sun was shining, so I opted for a pair of extremely short black gym shorts, my uncomfortable trusty Converse, and a Nike T-shirt. My hair was up in a ponytail. I toyed with it down, then up again, then down, until settling on up. It was hot, so it made sense.

When I'd returned home the night before, Brooke told me she planned to take me on a trip outside the big city to a place called Nikko. She arrived at Beth's apartment at 9 a.m. sharp. The trip was roughly an hour quicker by car than by train. As soon as I stepped outside the apartment and felt the humidity I was thankful for the air-conditioned car.

We eased into conversation. I wanted to know all about her life in Japan. She spoke in detail about the language barrier and how she was slowly trying to overcome it whilst trying not to be culturally ignorant. Japan was a very homogenous country. There was still a public stigma towards being a white English girl, but after she made some friends she felt more comfortable, and they helped her adjust to life in Tokyo.

The fashion still concerned her. She admitted she wasn't cool enough to pull off some of the outfits she saw in the shop windows, so she stuck with H&M for most of her clothing needs. She spoke about the culture: bowing instead of shaking hands, removing shoes before you enter someone's home, eating and drinking on trains and in the street was frowned upon, and chopstick etiquette was another thing all together.

Who knew you couldn't point your chopsticks at someone?

"I took up Japanese classes as soon as I got here. In the classroom there was a sign on the wall in giant gold letters, it said, *The golden rule is to be respectful.* It's more about being aware. I'd read it was easy to offend people, so I was conscious of that when I arrived."

She turned right onto another long winding road that went on for miles.

"Have you offended anyone?" I asked.

"Only once that I know of." Brooke squirmed.

"Bad?"

"When I first got here, I went to a high-end sushi restaurant, and the sushi pieces were quite large. I was still getting used to chopsticks, so I cut the sushi piece in half. The chef looked at me like I'd just told him his cooking was terrible, and he muttered something under his breath."

"What did you do wrong?" I wasn't following.

"I didn't understand at first, but the waiter informed me that splitting sushi is seen as incredibly rude to a sushi chef. How was I to know that?"

"Seriously? I had no idea either."

"I made it worse; I placed my chopsticks in my bowl of rice, just to hold them whilst I had a drink."

"Okay . . . What's so bad about that?" I laughed.

"It symbolises death."

I almost choked on my water. "No, it doesn't?"

"Yep, at funerals in Japanese culture, people stick chopsticks in the rice facing upwards during rituals. It reminds them of death, and it's bad luck. Obviously, I had no idea, but it tipped the sushi chef over the edge; he began ranting and refused to serve us after that."

"You're kidding, right?"

"Nope, the guy next to me was not as conservative and found the whole thing rather funny. I haven't been back to that place since." She cringed.

"I'm not surprised." I could picture Brooke's face going increasingly flushed in that situation. It made me laugh.

"It's not funny."

"It's a little funny. Did your dad not have anything to say about that?" Her face dropped. It was the first time either of us had mentioned her father, or as I preferred to think of him—the devil. He was the elephant in the room, and I wanted to address the subject early on.

"Not really."

The conversation ended swiftly.

We spoke about different Netflix series and flicked through my Spotify playlists only to discover she knew the words to every song I assumed wasn't mainstream. I informed her of the recent drama in my life regarding Danielle's pregnancy. She asked about the firm and how everyone was doing, which ultimately resulted in a twenty-minute conversation about the bizarre things Paula had been doing, including her most recent purchase—a parrot.

"She bought a parrot?"

"Yes. It's green and yellow, and she called it Moira."

"Why Moira?" Brooke asked.

"The previous owner was obsessed with the TV show *Schitt's Creek*. The parrot just keeps saying, 'Moira Rose, Moira Rose', repeatedly."

Brooke burst out laughing. "That's brilliant."

"She's been trying to teach Moira to say, *Holly's a shit bag*, so I get that every time she calls." She found that amusing too, but I was more than happy to see her laugh at my expense.

The SatNav indicated we were thirty minutes from our destination. I'd brought supplies in the form of Tokyo Banana Rolls and Kit Kats, but not just any flavoured Kit Kats. They were double cookie flavour, which happened to be my favourite. Beth went through a phase of trying the 300+ flavours produced in Japan. She'd often sent me care packages of the flavours she hated, so as her best friend I could experience them too. Ginger ale was the worst, oh, and cherry blossom. Eww.

"Is it strange driving in Japan?" I asked because she seemed so confident with it.

"Not really. I got used to it pretty quickly. The signs are in English as well as Japanese. That's a huge help. Although, the danger signs aren't, which is strange. If I see a yellow triangle, I avoid it."

"Best way."

My phone buzzed from the passenger door compartment; it was Paula. The thing about Paula was, if I ignored her, she would continue to ring. If I ignored her more than three times, she'd be on the next flight to Tokyo to scold me in person.

"I have to take this."

"Of course." Brooke smiled.

"Hi, Paula."

"Holly! Thank god you answered. I have an update on the Wilde case." She sounded frantic.

"Okay, what's going on?" I didn't like the sound of her tone.

"The assailant's appointed lawyer has come back claiming it was self-defence. They're bumping up the first hearing at the magistrates' to next week."

"Next week, you've got to be kidding me. I'm not even in the country! Can we push for an adjournment?"

"I spoke with Mr. West, he doesn't think we have the grounds to do so." When Mr. West had an opinion on something, he was normally right.

"Okay . . ." Think Holly, think. "You attend court with another lawyer; take Brownstone. He owes me a favour. Once you get there, immediately seek to adjourn."

"On what grounds?" Paula asks.

"In order to obtain further evidence. If we do that, we can agree on a later date when I'll be back in the UK."

"Okay, but it's Judge Baron. She knows you. She knows your tricks."

"Shit!"

Judge Baron was a tough old cookie. She was in her early sixties. She was ruthless, and she knew every trick in the book. I'd tried to battle with her on numerous occasions to no avail, losing your clients case in front of Baron was a disaster for everyone; her sentences were worse than most.

"Do you think it'll go to the crown court?" Paula asked.

"I don't think so; we have two witness testimonies, CCTV footage of the brawl, X-rays, and pictures of Mr. Wilde directly after the assault, them pleading self-defence is barbaric." Mr. Wilde was viciously attacked for his watch and wallet after a night out with friends. He suffered a fracture of the orbital bone cavity in his eye as well as a skull fracture resulting in three operations and severe scarring.

The assailant claims he was acting in self-defence, but numerous suspects saw him attacking Mr. Wilde unprovoked. The evidence mounted to a quick win, but law was more complicated than that. The assailant then claimed he was sexually assaulted by Mr. Wilde at the urinal, and when they exited the pub he was overcome with emotion and attacked him.

"Did you manage to speak to the witness regarding the alleged sexual assault?" I rubbed at my forehead; I was off the clock, but never truly.

"No, they declined to comment."

"Brilliant." I inhaled deeply. "Okay, here's what we're going to do. I need you to go back through the evidence. The facts aren't compelling enough on their own. If they go with the sexual assault plea that gives them a solid argument; he won't get off scot-free, but it throws the whole testimony under scrutiny. Mr. Wilde frequents The Tavern often. I want you to get witness testimony from anyone that's ever shared a urinal with him. There must be several locals that would be willing to give character evidence."

What else—

"We can't alter the facts, but we can steer them in a different direction. Look at the defence files and see who the assailant went to school with. See who he works with. Is there any sign of sexual assault in his background? Any false allegations? Any rumours about him being gay? I understand he's married with a wife and child. If he has so much as sniffed another man's aftershave inappropriately I want to know about it." I paused, trying to recall all the facts of the case.

"If we go with the narrative that the assailant has a history of homosexual behaviour and in turn he is the one that instigated the contact in the urinal, we can claim Mr. Wilde backed away, he left swiftly, and the assailant's ego was bruised, so he followed him into the parking lot and beat the crap out of him and tried to make it look like a mugging by taking his watch and wallet."

"That's good. I like that." I could hear Paula tapping away on her laptop keys at the other end. "Aren't we admitting to some activity in the urinal then? Mr. Wilde claims there was no such assault, and he barely even remembers this man being in the toilet," Paula questioned.

"If that's the case, what is the motive? As far as I'm aware the assailant has nothing but a petty theft and a few speeding fines on his record. He's not well-off, but he's not struggling, so there was no real need to steal his wallet and his watch. He's a family man with no previous history of violence." When I said it out loud it made the case so much more complex. A case was never as straightforward as I thought it was going to be. Even when I believed wholeheartedly someone was telling the truth, proving it was the hard part.

"What was his motive? Not the picture we're creating, but the actual motive," Paula asked.

"I have no idea, but if you stumble across that whilst you're looking let me know."

"Okay. I think I know where to start. I'll get Mr. West to contact Baron; they go way back, maybe he can get the court date moved. You need to be at the magistrates'. You're the one who knows this case; it's not going to bode well for Mr. Wilde if you're not here."

"Agreed." I knew Paula would have the first email sent before we even got off the phone. She was efficient, and that's why I loved working with her. "Oh, one more thing, just a hunch I have, but check the assailant's history of love interests. Is he on any dating sites? Any social media evidence of wrongdoing? Has he ever cheated on his wife?" I asked.

It was a long shot, but there was something niggling away at me that I couldn't put my finger on.

"Why?" Paula questioned.

"Just a hunch."

"Oh, one of those gut feelings that appear to be 100 percent true. I hate it when you do that. It's like some weird superpower." I could practically hear her eyes rolling back in her head.

"Well, I can't fly or lift cars with one hand, so give me this one."

"Okay, I'll get back to work. Call you later!"

The road ahead curved off to the right. As we rounded the corner, I turned my attention back to Brooke. I could see her smirking out of the corner of my eye.

"Sorry about that."

"No problem. How many times has she called you on this holiday?"

"Just two times so far."

"Let me guess, you told her to, 'call you if she needed anything'."

"No . . . not at all." I looked out the window to hide my smile.

"You're work obsessed. Sounds like an interesting case though. I miss that."

"The cases?"

"Yeah, the fact that no day is the same. I liked solving problems. Searching through the evidence was my favourite part." There was a brief pause. She opened her mouth to speak but decided against it.

"What were you going to say?"

"I also miss watching you in action." Her body froze. Her hands gripped the steering wheel tighter. I could feel the tension radiating from her stiff posture.

She was uncomfortable.

It felt like we were both carefully selecting our words because the slightest hiccup would do us both harm. After a few seconds of silence she justified her comment.

"Hearing you talk reminded me of all the times I watched you present evidence, or advise clients, or just debate with Mr. West on the best approach to a case. I found it all fascinating. I found you fascinating."

She didn't take her eyes off the road. She found me fascinating—The words echoed in my mind. As we approached the sign for Nikko, her body loosened. For months I had longed to hear her voice and witness her beauty in the flesh and not just through the photos on my phone I couldn't bring myself to delete.

She found *me* fascinating.

Such a simple sentence evoked deep emotion.

*

"The national park?" I observed the sign as I climbed out of the car. "This looks pretty."

"I figured you don't get to experience a lot of this in London, so why not experience the glorious Japanese countryside."

Brooke spun around with her arms outstretched and her head raised towards the sky. The smile on her face was enough to brighten my day; I could go home now.

"What's in the backpack?" She'd launched the small black bag over her shoulders when we left the car.

"A few supplies. You'll see."

"Wait, is that a *Finding Nemo* keyring?" I went to grab it to take a closer look. She spun like lightening and swatted my hand away.

"Don't you pick on my keyring." She smirked. "I know it's childish, but I saw it in Tokyu Hands, and I couldn't resist."

"Didn't they have an *Avatar* one?" I asked.

"Unfortunately not." She eyed me suspiciously.

"It's my favourite film too, remember?" I played it down, but either way I would've remembered.

We began our climb up the stone steps into the temple complex. The whole area was covered in gardens and manicured forest. There was greenery as far as the eye could see. Following the path upwards we arrived at a large clearing. I followed Brooke through a gate and into a Japanese-style garden called Shōyō-en. The spring greenery throughout the garden looked beautiful. Surrounding the pond were vines of white wisteria; pointing that out to Brooke was my only contribution. It was the one plant I knew for certain.

The next stop involved walking down a sloping incline from the clearing towards Toshogu Shrine. Over a dozen old heavily embellished shrines were located in the forest; the whole experience felt enchanting. They were lavishly decorated and well preserved.

"This is one of Japan's most decorated shrine complexes. I think it's from the 1600s, which is crazy when you think about it," Brooke said.

I observed the intricate wooden carvings of animals, including elephants and cats. The gold detail and moss covered stone lanterns were unique.

"Would you like to hike? There are a couple of waterfalls in the area." Brooke asked.

My feet were screaming, *Don't do it to me*. Had I been better informed of the day's itinerary I wouldn't have picked Converse as my footwear of choice. Brooke saw my concerned look and glanced down at my feet.

"Probably should've told you the plan was to hike. We can turn back if you like?"

"No, it's fine; lead the way." I wasn't about to let some slim toed trainers ruin my day.

The further we climbed, the terrain became more rugged and mountainous. We tried to follow the tree lined routes to avoid the suns direct rays. Brooke pulled two caps from her backpack, which was the first I'd seen of the mystery supplies.

The first part of the trail was predominantly flat. I was thankful for the cool breeze that rippled through the trees every so often. In the distance I heard the tumbling and crashing of water as it hit rocks. We must be close. Brooke led the way for most of the walk. I fixated on how her shiny calves tightened and her bum clenched with every extended stride. What a pervert.

The waterfall was flanked by yellow and red trees. A fellow hiker told us to follow the river upstream to enjoy the more impressive views of the water rushing towards Lake Chuzenji. We grabbed a bottle of water from a small food stand and continued on our way. Brooke estimated the trail would take no more than three hours. That would be enough time to get a taste of the national park.

We marched through the marshy plains and long grass of Nikko for over an hour until we reached Yumoto Onsen. It was a hot spring town. The scenery was magnificent, but the town looked a little run down, abandoned almost. When we got closer I noticed the crowds gathering around the foot bath.

A gentleman approached and ushered us over to the wooden structure.

"This is the perfect place to soothe tired legs after hiking, please, enjoy." He bowed and moved on to the next group of hikers. We removed our socks and shoes; as soon as my feet hit the warm water my whole body loosened.

"Why is the water white?" Brooke asked.

"Sulphur, I think; it's what makes it so smooth. I read about the hot springs on the flight over." We both dipped our hands deep into the water and began bathing our arms and legs.

"I've never actually been here before." Brooke looked beyond the hot springs into the vast natural surroundings.

"I thought you knew where we were going?" I asked suspiciously.

"Nope, I knew up until a point, but I'm not entirely sure how we got here." She giggled.

"That's good to know. I don't think I'll be using you as a tour guide again," I joked. I wasn't concerned. It couldn't be that difficult to find our way back—I hoped.

The fatigue I felt from hiking for two hours disappeared as we gathered our belongings and left, but first we ate some soba noodles to refuel. Brooke handed me a fresh pair of socks (another item from her mystery backpack). I was thankful because I'd had to peel my sweaty ones off. I was concerned that my feet were now warm. Converse don't agree with warm swollen feet.

We continued trekking for 4.3 miles. I know that because my Apple Watch told me so. My feet were starting to sting, and as much as I loved Brooke's company, the only thing getting me through was the thought of being sat in the car on the drive home.

*

It was 6 p.m. as the sun dropped behind the mountains in the distance. The still humid air became more bearable once the sun disappeared. The clothes on my back were so wet that it was pointless wearing them. The Nike T-shirt hung from my shoulder. Luckily my sports bra passed as trail appropriate clothing. Had I opted for fancier underwear that morning I'd have been screwed.

The trees all looked familiar now. The people we passed on the trails became less frequent. The wildlife started to appear. We saw a deer drinking from a river, which was delightful and very sweet. Immediately after, I saw a sign that said, *Beware of bears*—which was less sweet.

"You don't think there are actually bears in here, do you?" I asked.

Brooke looked alarmed when she noticed the sign I was referring to. "Erm . . ."

"What?"

"There was an article a few months ago about a man that got attacked by a black bear in Nikko."

My gulp was audible. "You're joking, right?"

"Nope, I wish I was."

"I wish you hadn't told me that."

Suddenly, every crack of a branch or bristle of leaves caused me to jump. Deer I could deal with, monkeys absolutely, bears, certainly not.

"Are we lost? I feel like we're lost?" Each way we turned looked the same.

"Didn't we already come this way? I feel like I saw that tree on its side about a mile ago. We've gone round in a circle, haven't we?" It was my fault. I'd barely paid attention to the signs. I assumed Brooke knew where she was going.

"Possibly. I'm sure we were supposed to follow the signs to Toshogu Shrine and from there to Nikko Station, but I haven't seen either one of those signs for a while now." Brooke sighed.

We'd picked up a map before entering the park, but the map was useless because we didn't know where on the map we were located.

Brooke pulled her phone from her pocket. "It's dead. Do you have yours?"

"I told you I left it in the car because I have no pockets." I kicked at a rock in frustration. "Well, this is just great. We are completely lost." I flapped my hands.

"I'm sorry, but you could've been paying attention too. It's not all my fault," Brooke claimed.

"I'm not the one who lives in Japan. If you'd have told me to pay attention I would've done, but you didn't." I slumped on the nearest rock and began undoing my laces.

"What are you doing?" Brooke asked.

"I'm walking barefoot; if I walk another mile in these trainers my toes are going to fall off."

"Is that my fault too?" Brooke scowled.

"You didn't tell me we'd be hiking the Pacific Crest Trail." The PC Trail between Mexico and Canada was 2600 miles long, so it was a dramatic comparison, but I was angry.

"I have no idea what that is, but I can sense your sarcasm, and I don't appreciate it." She folded her arms and sulked. If I wasn't stuck in the middle of a forest surrounded by killer bears, I'd probably have laughed.

"Can we keep walking, please? We probably have three hours before it's pitch black. Then we are officially a black bear's dinner," I said.

"They prefer grass and fruit to humans." Brooke stuck her tongue out and stomped off in the opposite direction. "I doubt they eat sarky English lawyers."

"This way, Brooke. We just came from that direction."

"No, we didn't."

"Yes, we did. The rock was on my left when we walked up," I pointed out.

"I don't think it was."

"Trust me; it was. I don't think we can rely on your sense of direction anymore."

"Fine. When we're lost it'll be your fault this time." Brooke spun around and stomped back past me with a vengeance.

"We're already lost!" I yelled.

CHAPTER EIGHT

The shades of greenery turned darker as we made another right turn. Our logic was simple: don't turn the same direction more than twice in a row. It wasn't bulletproof, but we figured it would stop us going around in a circle.

We were high above Lake Chuzenjiko. The views were spectacular. Unfortunately, they were shrouded by the uncertainty of the situation. We'd barely spoken a word to each other since I started walking barefoot, which felt like a long time ago. Surprisingly, my feet had become numb to the rocky pathways. I doubted I'd be able to walk the following day, but making it out alive was my main concern.

Only two hikers passed us, one didn't speak a word of English, and the other ran with headphones. We tried to flag him down like hitchhikers, but he completely ignored us. Brooke understood Japanese to a degree, but not enough to converse effectively with the older gentleman we encountered. He spoke in a completely different dialect than she was used to. He did however make a triangular sign with his hands; we weren't sure if that meant warning or—

"Tent!" I yelled.

Brooke looked up.

"Brooke look over there—a campsite."

We practically launched ourselves down the slope towards the sign that read, *Shobugahama Camping Site*.

The campground sat on the edge of Lake Chuzenjiko, and the best news, it was open and bustling with campers.

"Thank god! I'm sure someone here can tell us how to get back." I sighed. Relief washed over me.

A middle-aged man with a goatee and a waterproof cap approached us. He looked friendly, and by the looks of his sweat-sodden outfit he'd been hiking all day too. He glanced down at my feet, which were now filthy and sore.

"English?" He asked.

Was it that obvious?

I nodded. He bowed politely. "Welcome, do you have a reservation?"

"No, we're actually lost, and we need help finding our way back to our car," I said.

"Where is your car?" he asked.

"Somewhere near Nikko station," Brooke answered.

He wiped his forehead and stood with his hand on his hip contemplating something.

"There is a bus back to Nikko station." My face lit up. ". . . but they have stopped running for the night. The next one leaves at 8:30 a.m." My hopes were shattered once again.

"Oh. Is there no other way to get back?" Brooke asked.

"You could walk," he suggested, ". . . but it will take you approximately five hours."

"Oh." I wanted to cry.

"I don't think you can walk five hours with no shoes." He glanced at my feet once again; now I was self-conscious.

The man pointed to a small wooden hut at the other side of the campground.

"If you go to the shop, maybe they can provide you with a tent for the night . . . and some socks."

"Thank you."

"*Dōitashimashite*." He bowed again and continued towards the lake.

"You're welcome?" I looked at Brooke to clarify.

"You learn quick." It was a lucky guess.

The smell of food overwhelmed my senses. People were setting up their fire pits in every direction. There were women making giant bowls of rice, men cutting meat, and children turning fish on the portable cookers with chopsticks; it was a real family affair. They were cooking as though they weren't camping, but in the warmth of their own homes. The smell of butter chicken caused my stomach to tighten. I was so hungry.

The woman behind the counter in the shop looked displeased to be there, which was unusual. I'd never had an experience with impolite locals before. She rushed through serving the customers before us; maybe the shop was due to close.

The shop sold a range of vital necessities. I purchased a grey hoodie with a green mountain logo on the front. I preferred it to the one with bears inside a warning triangle. I grabbed a large bottle of water, some toothpaste, a toothbrush, and most importantly teriyaki flavoured crisps.

"I'm sorry," Brooke said as she glanced over my shoulder at the limited chocolate section.

"Me too. I shouldn't have yelled."

"It's fine. I would've yelled too. Here, I found these. Might be better than what's currently on your feet." Brooke handed me a pair of croc-style slip-on shoes in green. "Kind of matches the hoodie too." She ran her hand down my arm and wandered to the other side of the shop to look for more supplies.

When my hands were full, I approached the woman behind the counter. "Excuse me, do you have any tents available, please?"

"No," she replied sharply.

"None at all?"

"This is the summer; we are fully booked until August." She began pulling items from the counter and scanning them one by one with urgency.

"Oh, so there's no way we can hire a tent?"

"All tents are gone. You book early or you bring your own tent."

"But we just walked for five hours straight, and we have no way of getting back until the morning. Surely you can—" She cut me off.

"No tents. There is another campground that way; try that one. They might have availability for you." The woman whose name badge read, *Sakura*, pointed towards the map on the wall. "Total is 8020 yen."

"Thank you for nothing." Brooke grabbed her chocolate and left. The day couldn't get any worse.

*

When I slipped on the crocs I understood what walking on clouds really meant. They gave me the burst of energy I needed to chase after Brooke. She was quickly making her way across the campsite.

"Brooke, wait."

"What are we supposed to do now? Sleep in the forest? She didn't need to be so mean," Brooke cried clenching her fists. When I reached her side, I dropped my trainers, which she automatically kicked. "Hey, what did they ever do to you?"

"What are we supposed to do, Holly?"

The words were forced through clenched teeth, her voice strained. She threw her arms up.

"Nobody's going to help us. We'll get eaten before the sun comes up. My phone's dead, so I can't even let anyone know where we are or that I'm safe. If my dad doesn't hear from me, the police will be out searching for me by midnight. This was supposed to be a nice day, and I've ruined it."

I placed my hands on her shoulders, closing the gap between us. "Hey."

She shook her head, so I placed both my hands on her cheeks. It was instinct to swipe away the tears.

"Look at me. I'll figure something out."

"How?" She sobbed.

I touched my forehead to Brooke's, running my hands down her arms and entangling my fingers with hers.

"Trust me. Just breathe." Sucking in breath, I let the space around me fade into the background. Her eyes were focused on mine, her chest falling into the same rhythm as my own, and I wanted to kiss her.

There was an audible cough to our right that immediately broke the intimacy between us.

"Sorry to interrupt," said a woman with a yellow beanie and a checked grey shirt.

"I overheard you in the store. Me and my friends over there." She turned and pointed towards a group of thirty-somethings; they waved back emphatically. "We feel bad for you, and we have a spare tent if you need a place to stay?"

"Seriously?" Brooke beamed.

"Sure." The woman's smile was warm.

"That's extremely kind of you. Thank you so much," I said.

Brooke grabbed my hand and squeezed it tightly.

"My name is Hana. You guys are?"

"I'm Brooke. This is Holly."

"Nice to meet you. Do you want me to walk you through the camp amenities?"

We both nodded enthusiastically.

Hana showed us to the bathing facilities. I'd never been so happy to see clean water and soap. The cooking facilities were a little further down, although it seemed nobody at the camp needed those. She pointed out that the shop had Wi-Fi and charging ports. Brooke put her phone on charge for long enough to let her dad know she was impromptu camping this evening with her friend Takara. I didn't ask who that was, and it technically wasn't any of my business, but I knew she wasn't a lesbian lawyer from the UK, or her dad would be driving up to Nikko immediately.

I took the opportunity to send Beth a message and let her know I was still alive—unless the bears came for me in the night—She didn't appreciate that part. Her response was, *I am not telling your parents you've been mauled by a bear, so you better get home in one piece.*

Hana and her friends were very hospitable. Their group included four tents. There were three couples and two single women who'd become friends after finding out their boyfriend had been seeing them both at the same time for almost a year. I liked the dynamic.

They allowed us to eat with them, freshly made yakisoba and Yaki Onigiri, which was essentially balls of rice grilled on the BBQ with seasoning. They were unbelievable.

They offered us two spare camping chairs, and we cozied up next to the roaring fire. The panic from the day's events had completely disappeared. The group were fairly local, but thankfully spoke fluent English. They asked questions about the UK and what it was like to live in London. They found it just as fascinating as I found Japan, which was strange to me, but it goes to show England does have some appeal.

One of the women was a lawyer, so we spoke about our respective careers, and the whole time I could feel Brooke watching me. She made me nervous. What was she thinking? Did she revel in the excitement of us sharing a tent in the same way I did? It was polite to partake in conversation with the people who had so graciously provided us with a place to stay, but all I could think about was being alone with Brooke.

The night drew to a close. Hana pulled supplies from everyone's tents for ours, and once she was finished it looked like one of those cosy forts you make as a child using all the sofa cushions and your bed linens. I used the bathroom to freshen up and climbed into our fort for the night.

The distant chatter of other tents could be heard, but the birds singing in the trees overpowered any other sound. The double sleeping bag wasn't a necessity, it was still roughly nineteen degrees outside, so we weren't going to freeze to death.

"This sure beats sleeping outside," I whispered.

Brooke turned to face me. The glow of the lights outside brought her face into focus. God, she was beautiful.

"Did you put the padlock on the tent?" She buried herself deeper into the sleeping bag.

"Yes."

"Are you sure?"

"Yes, why?"

"The bears, you heard the stories those guys were telling."

"Do you think a bear is going to care if the tent is locked? If it wants to eat us, it's getting in regardless. I'm sure one swipe of its claws would cut straight through this material." I bashed against the nylon waterproof fabric. I wasn't making myself feel any better.

"Thanks for that." Brooke said.

The tent was relatively small, in an outdoorsy type shop it would probably be described as a two-man tent. It was big enough to fit a double inflatable bed and not much more, but I was okay with that.

I stared unwaveringly into Brooke's eyes. She smirked. In that moment I wished I could trade my "hunch" superpower Paula claimed I possessed for a mind reading one. It would be invasive, but I wouldn't be opposed to it. I analysed and gathered evidence for a living. It was my job to find out the truth, to expose the truth even, but in my personal life I found that so much harder.

"Can I ask you something?" Brooke asked.

"Of course."

She toyed with the zipper on the edge of the sleeping bag, her gaze meeting mine then dropping again.

"If our circumstances had been different, do you think we would've made it?"

"Why are you asking that?" I leant up on my elbow.

"It's been two years; a lot changes. I guess I'm just curious." She smiled softly.

"Well, it depends."

"On what?" Brooke asked.

"When you saw my name light up on your phone last night, did it still give you butterflies?" The comment took a moment to register. I saw the change in her eyes when it did, when she recalled the words she'd written in her letter.

"Yes." Her response was barely above a whisper and preluded a soft sigh.

"Well, there you go. There is no doubt in my mind."

"None at all?" Brooke raised her eyebrow.

I reached forwards and tucked a curl of hair behind her ear. She leaned into my hand. The feel of her skin was warm and soft. It was so quiet I could hear her breathing accelerate.

"There are only two things in life I am certain of; one is death... and the other is my love for *you*," I whispered.

Brooke reached for the tassels dangling from my new mountain hoodie. She pulled at them softly, twirling them between her fingers. She was distracting herself from the tension. I knew because I could feel it building, with each second in silence the air grew thicker. I could feel the lump in my throat when I swallowed. The beat of my heart was banging so hard against my chest it was visible. The slightest touch of her fingertips as they brushed against my neck made me shiver.

I reached forwards and trailed my fingers down the side of her cheek to her lips. She pulled lightly on the strings of my hooded sweater, bringing my lips closer to hers. We were so close I could feel the warmth of her breath. She brushed her lips against mine. The anticipation of the kiss was too much to handle. Our lips moulded gently. It was tender and slow. Her hand caressed the back of my neck, edging my body closer to her.

The warmth of her body radiated through her clothes. I heaved the cover back as her hand slipped down to cradle the side of my neck. My hands had never been so unsteady as I gripped her waist. The soft touch of her skin was like velvet in my hand.

"We can't." Brooke pressed her forehead to mine, rolling to the right slightly, so her lips weren't directly in line with mine.

"Why?" I asked.

"It'll only make things harder when . . ." I kissed the side of her temple, moving slowly down her cheek, kissing the line of her neck from her ear to her collarbone. ". . . you leave." She sighed, half pleasure, half disappointment. I could sense her eagerness to continue, but maybe she was right. Was she trying to save me the heartache, or herself? Maybe both?

She stared into my eyes with a dreamlike intensity I will never forget, but the reality of the situation was apparent. As much as I wanted one night with her, I knew in my heart it wouldn't change anything.

Brooke lived in Japan.

I lived in England.

She still chose her family over me.

Those were the facts.

I yearned for a life that would never be mine.

CHAPTER NINE

The next morning the lake's shores and surrounding mountains were so clearly exposed I could see for miles. There was something soothing about waking up in the wilderness surrounded by the rattling of leaves and birds tweeting above. The sounds reminded me of a Spotify playlist.

I freshened up at the bathing area and enjoyed a morning coffee coupled with some French toast courtesy of our new camping friends.

"How did you sleep?" I asked Brooke.

"Good. You?"

It was torture. Actual torture in the form of sexual tension. I barely slept for the first two hours after our close encounter. She'd fallen asleep first, and as my eyelids finally felt the weight of the day's events, she turned over to face me and wrapped her arm around my torso, just above my pelvic bone. She wasn't conscious in her action. She was just reaching for some comfort, but her hand moved up and down causing my hoody to ride up and her soft skin to brush against mine. That was enough to stop sleep from pulling me under.

"Erm . . . yeah. I slept okay."

Lie number one.

"Do you want to talk about last night?" Brooke whispered.

I shrugged. "I'm not sure there's anything to say."

Lie number two.

There was a lot to say. Novels upon novels could be written with the things I wanted to say, but it was ineffectual because I would always be powerless to the constraints placed on us.

"Oh." She recoiled. "Okay."

Brooke charged her phone for thirty minutes, and when it sprung to life the notifications immediately came pinging through. As I walked behind her, I noticed the caller ID on her screen; it was Takara.

Brooke didn't answer.

"Has she been calling you all night?"

"I probably should have told her I'd told my dad I was camping with her. She'll be confused," Brooke said.

"Why would she need to know? Surely your dad's not calling all your friends to check up on you. You're twenty-seven years old," I scoffed. He was controlling enough when she was twenty-five. I hoped for her sake, he'd loosened the reigns.

"No, of course not, but I know Takara through her dad working with mine. We get invited to their house a lot for dinner as a family."

The whole thing was strange to me. Brooke seemed cagey, but it wasn't my place to pry.

"Whatever you say," I replied sarcastically. I shouldn't have, but a bitterness still stung whenever I thought about her dad. I would never forgive him for taking away our chance to be happy.

"My dad doesn't control my life anymore, Holly, before you start getting on your high horse." Anymore being the key word. "I'm looking at moving out in a couple of months."

"Good for you."

"Has anyone ever told you how annoying your sarcasm is?"

"Yes."

The conversation was interrupted by Hana, but I did want to know more about the moving out thing, so I made a mental note to broach that subject on the car ride home.

"We're going kayaking today, if you guys would like to join?" Hana pointed towards the rest of the gang who were dragging large yellow kayaks towards the lake.

"That sounds amazing, but I do have to get back for work tonight. It was only supposed to be a day trip." Brooke smiled politely.

"No problem. We are up here for the next seven days. If you guys fancy coming back, just let us know." Brooke and Hana exchanged phone numbers. It was polite; maybe they could be friends, but as far as intimate tent encounters go, me and Brooke didn't need another.

"I would take the bus back if I were you. There's going to be a heatwave today, and five hours trekking will be tough," Hana pointed out. Duly noted.

"Thank you." My feet thanked her too.

The journey back to Nikko Station took over an hour. My phone still had 10 percent battery when we got back to the car. I had three missed calls from Paula and five text messages: one from my mum, two from Beth, each growing in urgency until I'd managed to reach her. In the last text message she mellowed out.

Beth
Holly, why aren't you answering your phone?

Beth
Holly, where are you?

Beth

You're scaring me now. PLEASE don't have been kidnapped.

Beth

Let me know when you get back to the car, so I know you survived the night. Also, super glad you didn't get kidnapped by her crazy ass dad, because I've literally just had a manicure and I wouldn't want to ruin it by murdering him. FYI—I don't know if you know, but I'm pregnant, and this kind of stress isn't good for the baby. I'll be telling her or him all about this when she or he is older. Bad Auntie. I still love you though.

Beth's message made me laugh out loud. I replied quickly, making her aware I would fill her in on all the details when I arrived home. There were more email notifications than I cared to admit; I muted those straight away. My mum wanted to know if I would bring my dad some sencha and matcha tea home because he'd seen on a travelling programme that Japan considered tea to be sacred, and some spiel about Buddhism and personal fulfilment. Dad was on a new hype, fun.

Paula's messages were similar to Beth's until Beth had obviously informed her I had not been kidnapped or eaten alive. She requested I call her tomorrow, which would be today. My phone started ringing like clockwork. I sent it to voicemail. Work could wait. I was on vacation.

"Can I ask you something?" I thought I might as well dive straight in.

"Here we go." Brooke sighed.

"What does that mean?"

"I could tell you wanted to ask back at the campsite. You barely spoke to me on the bus, so go on. What is it?"

Wow, the attitude wasn't necessary. "Never mind." I folded my arms.

"Seriously, Holly?"

"It doesn't matter now."

"You're like a child." Brooke was visibly annoyed.

"Says you."

"Are you a Lawyer, or a five-year-old?"

Hurtful.

"That's rich coming from someone who asks for her father's permission to stay out overnight."

"Wow, real nice. How long have you been holding that one in?"

I turned towards the window. Looking into the expanse of trees gave me a distraction, well not really. Out the corner of my eye I could see her gripping the steering wheel so tightly the veins in her hands were visible.

After five minutes she broke the silence.

"FYI, I don't ask my dad's permission, okay. It's just polite to let him know. He worries."

"Right." It sounded all too familiar.

"He wants me to move out. He's happy I'm starting to stand on my own two feet and live my life."

"Uh, huh." You keep protecting him just like you always have, I thought.

"He was the one who suggested it. He said I should move in with Takara. It was his idea."

"Have you heard yourself?" I snapped.

"What?"

"You do realise I deal with people who are in serious denial every single day?"

"I'm not in denial."

"You scream denial." I laughed. She didn't like that.

"You're such an asshole." She huffed.

Maybe so, but I had a point, and now I was beyond annoyed. "Why did you even get my attention in Shibuya? You should have just ignored me."

It would have made the whole trip ten times easier. I could have left never having seen her, and my brain would be less scrambled than it was now.

"Do you really think that I could not see you?"

I shrugged.

"Do you think I could go about my day knowing you were in the same country as me? In the same goddamn building as me? You think I could just ignore you? You're crazy," she yelled.

"You should have," I said it with venom on my tongue, but I didn't mean it. I didn't want her to ignore me; I wanted the complete opposite.

"Yeah, well I couldn't, okay?"

"Why not? Why make things complicated? Look at us now." I flung my hand out and accidentally whacked my fingers on the dashboard. "Fuck. Ouch."

"Because . . . I fucking love you. Isn't it obvious?"

She still loved me? *Oh.*

"I never stopped loving you. Do you think for one second I'd be able to sleep, eat, or focus on anything knowing you were within touching distance and I didn't do anything about it? You're fucking delusional, and I hate you for it. I hate you for this, for making me feel out of control."

The words registered. The throbbing in my hand added a heightened sensory element. I gripped my fingers tightly in my other hand, trying not to make it a big deal.

"Pull over," I said.

She ignored me.

"Pull over . . . please."

There was a turnoff ahead. Perfect timing. Brooke pulled onto the long tree-lined street. The trees towered so high it was impossible to see through the top of them. I felt cocooned; the road was surprisingly quiet, void of any life. We sat for a moment in silence with only the humming of the engine as background noise.

"You don't love me." I sighed deeply. I used my good hand to rub the frown lines on my forehead. "If you loved me, you'd never have left."

There it was, the elephant in the room. The words I'd wanted to say every single day for two years. They came out winey. I hated that. I wanted to say them again, but cooler, calmer, more like I'd grown as a person and accepted our fate, but instead I came off suppressed and pathetic.

"You know that's not true."

Brooke turned off the ignition. She pinched the bridge of her nose. There were tears visible. I pretended to consider her words, but I couldn't believe them, not fully. I held my breath as I waited for her to speak again.

"Holly," Brooke whispered. Eyebrows raised, she lifted her gaze to meet mine. There was an intensity there I'd never felt before. I was used to being in control, but I felt powerless to her. My feelings for her crippled me more than I'd thought possible.

In the shadow of the trees her face was so close to mine I could smell the campfire from the night before on her clothes. I could smell the fresh perfume Hana had kindly allowed her to use on her neck. The scent was fruity and refreshing, a scent unrecognisable to me on Hana, but on Brooke it smelt amazing.

Suddenly, I felt her lips, her tongue searching for mine, the intimacy of last night's kiss was no longer present; this was different. I felt her body pulsate, and the passionate yearning for my own as she reached her arms down unclipping her seatbelt and forcing me back. She clambered on top, straddling me with force.

The feeling of excitement and passion, but also fear, all mixed into one to create an adrenaline I'd never felt before. The throbbing in my finger disappeared once I gripped her waist and I was compelled to feel a different kind of pain: the ache of desire, the agony of longing for someone I could never have.

We clambered over the middle compartment of the SUV. Brooke first. I followed. She pulled my body towards her. Our lips never parted for more than a second. The back seat was large and relatively private due to the tinted windows. I was conscious the engine was off. The lack of air-conditioning for even a few minutes made the car feel like a sauna.

"It's hot in here," I mumbled.

"I don't care." Brooke removed her T-shirt followed by mine as our bodies began to feel the effects of a Japanese heatwave. I brushed her hair from her face, biting at her neck and her lip as I investigated her body.

This was a terrible idea; I knew it. Brooke probably knew it too, but in that moment my brain cancelled all conscious reasoning. Before I could think rationally we were naked and exploring each other's bodies in ways we'd never done before. The likely possibility we might get caught should have forced us to stop, but it only added to the excitement.

There was no stopping us now. There were no boundaries left to cross. Her legs were spread, her body applied pressure to mine; our perspiring bodies made the movement easier. I wanted to take control, but Brooke pinned my arms behind the back of the headrest and manoeuvred her hips forwards then back with the rhythm of a dancer.

"How do you do this to me?" Brooke asked.

I didn't respond.

"I can't resist you," she whispered in my ear. I clenched my hips and pressed against her with all the energy I could summon. I was defenceless, completely and utterly defenceless.

I couldn't stop, even if I'd wanted to.

*

After a restroom stop to freshen up and a quick improvised car valet Brooke dropped me back at Beth's apartment. When I entered, she stood with one hand on her hip and the other tapping the kitchen counter with her fingers like a parent whose child had just stayed out all night without permission.

"Hey." I smiled coyly.

"Hi." She looked me up and down. "You look like you've been having sex all day." As I got closer, she sniffed at me dramatically. "You even smell like sex!"

"I do not."

"Yes, you do, it's mixed with dirt, and camp fire fumes, but it's in there."

I waited for her to elaborate on her response.

"I want all the juicy details, but first, go and have a shower."

Huh. Details were good. Maybe the telling off would come at a later point.

I reached out and grabbed a strawberry from her fruit salad bowl. "You're so bossy when you're pregnant."

Beth was wearing some bizarre spandex leggings, and a crop top that showed off her enviable stomach muscles.

"Get used to it," she said whilst sticking her tongue out.

"Enjoy that flat stomach whilst you still can." I walked towards the bathroom chuckling. She threw a grape that bounced off the back of my head.

Ten minutes later I stood staring at my reflection in the bathroom mirror. A cold shower had given me the shock of a lifetime, but it soothed my warm sunburnt skin. I spat out a mouthful of toothpaste and nearly choked on my toothbrush when Beth burst into the bathroom.

"Okay, I'm bored of waiting," she said.

"Beth—have you heard of knocking? I could've been naked."

"I did knock, really quietly. And I lived with you in dorms. I've seen your naked ass numerous times, so don't flatter yourself. If I'd have wanted me some of that lesbian pussy in university, I could've had it." She gestured towards my vagina.

"I'm not going to deny it. I probably would have." I wiggled my eyebrows, jesting.

"God, could you imagine. It'd be like having sex with my sister. Eww." Beth pretended to vomit.

I cringed, and all was right with the world.

Beth slammed the toilet seat down and made herself comfortable.

"Why are you looking at me like that?" I laughed nervously.

"You know why. Did you?"

"Did I . . . go to law school? Did I . . . overindulge on the flight over here? Did I accidentally step on a wasp when I was ten and my foot swelled up like a balloon?"

"Oh my God, I got stung too! I think I was about seven though. I remember a bowl cut and a horrible carpet looking hat. Anyway, stop distracting me." She tapped her fingers on the sink.

"We didn't do anything last night, but—" I dropped the toothbrush back in the holder and tied the towel tighter around my body. "We did this morning." I scrunched my face and closed my eyes, waiting for the audible gasp, which came very quickly followed by.

"Are you fucking crazy?" Beth stood up and paced back and forth within the enclosed bathroom space.

"Probably," I admitted.

"You are. You're literally crazy. Do you like to cause yourself pain? There must be part of your brain that's wired up wrong. Instead of running for the hills like you should, or even better, getting eaten by a black bear, you fraternise with the enemy." She shook her head dramatically.

"I know." I sat on the edge of the bath. I found Beth ranting and pacing amusing, but I knew she was right.

"You don't know. You wouldn't do it if you *knew*. I didn't believe you'd be that much of an idiot. I thought you'd go and spend the day with her, realise she isn't all she's cracked up to be, and go home and marry Francesca, have beautiful little Italian babies with dark features to die for and live happily ever after." She used hand gestures channelling her inner Italian.

"What's the plan now? Are you going to keep sleeping with her for the next ten days, like some holiday romance, and just go back to London and move on? We both know you won't be able to do that," Beth said, still pacing.

"I'm damaged." It was true.

"Yep, agreed. Would I be surprised if your mum said she dropped you on your head as a child? No, not at this stage."

"What the fuck am I supposed to do?" I buried my head in my hands.

I wanted to only feel joy when I thought of Brooke, but the devastating pain she'd caused me emotionally was as fresh as the day she'd left.

"I'm basically the damaged parcel that turns up after the DPD driver has launched it around his van all day— That's me." I tried to laugh, but there were tears, which turned into this peculiar half laugh half cry I'd only ever experienced on one other occasion—when Brooke left the first time.

"You're not a damaged parcel."

"I am. They might as well send me back to the depo and launch me in the bin." I sulked.

Beth sat beside me on the edge of the bath and intertwined her fingers with mine.

"Look at me. You are not a damaged parcel." She tried to keep a straight face but burst out laughing after realising how stupid the analogy was.

"You're the box that comes with contents wrapped in bubble wrap and fragile tape; you're sturdy and strong, and not only perfectly pristine on the outside, but pretty beautiful on the inside too." Beth wiped a tear from my eye as I placed my head on her shoulder.

"So, I'm like a designer box then?"

"Exactly," she said. "Like what a new Louis Vuitton bag would come in."

"Okay, I can deal with that." I sniffled.

"On another note, was it good?"

I looked up at Beth. "Really?"

"What? You've already made the mistake. I just want to know if it was worth it." She shrugged.

I blushed.

"No need, I can tell by your face." She nudged me. "I know you want to tell me."

"It just felt right, as if we'd gone back in time, and nothing had changed between us. Even when we bickered, even then, I still felt more alive than I've ever felt with anyone else. It's hard to explain." I looked away, wiping the remaining tears from my face.

"You bickered, huh?"

"We had a full-blown argument about her dad being a controlling ass wipe."

"It does feel like we've gone back in time," Beth joked.

"Tell me about it? If experiencing heartbreak isn't painful enough the first time around, just do it again. God, I'm a moron!"

The shower may have washed away my sins, but I could still feel her on me.

"I know I can be harsh about the Brooke situation, but it's only because I love you, and I don't want to see you get hurt again. I promise to stop busting your chops about it. I'll always support whatever you choose to do, even if that means me having to pick up the pieces. You've got to live your life. Do what makes you happy in the moment," Beth said sincerely.

"Thank you."

"I suppose there are consequences to everything, but you're a big girl. My grandma used to say, 'If you fear the aftermath before you even attempt the thing that scares you, there will never be any consequences, and equally there will be no joy in life'." Beth squeezed my leg.

"I like that," I replied.

"Do you think you're going to see her again?" Beth asked encouragingly.

"She's working long shifts for the next two days, but she said she'd like to see me Friday."

"You're sure it's a good idea?"

"Probably not, but can I be honest with you?"

"Always." Beth smiled.

"If you told me Brooke was on the other side of Lake Biwa, but first I had to climb one hundred Mount Fujis and fight off one hundred black bears before swimming the forty miles across Lake Biwa to get to her. I would find a way." My voice was low but deliberate.

"That is the stupidest cutest thing I have ever heard you say." Beth stood up, ruffled my hair, and made for the door.

"I'm going to let you get changed. Me and you and a large tub of ice cream are going to sit and watch *My Best Friend's Wedding,* followed by *Pretty Woman,* and however many other films it takes until we eat ourselves into a Julia Roberts coma."

"Sounds like the perfect night."

CHAPTER TEN

If I was playing *Family Fortunes* and the host said, "Name the top five tourist places in Tokyo". I would certainly think of Mount Fuji. I'd never climbed it. On my numerous visits it was something I thought about, but never got around to doing.

Looking into it in depth, it was no mean feat. The need to prepare for all potential weather conditions and possible altitude sickness made me think twice about making the ten-hour trek. Luckily there was no way Beth was about to climb a mountain, so I was saved by the *baby*, not the bell.

After much debate we kept it within our itinerary but opted for views from afar. According to Ren, none were as picturesque as the views from Lake Kawaguchiko. We took the bus to the cable cars. From there we took a cable car to Tenjoyama Park. The view was stunning. We took the cable car to the top of Mount Tenjoyama. The view from the observatory deck was even more impressive. A few small clouds passed by the peak of Fuji until it was obscured no more, and I was satisfied with seeing it from afar. I didn't need to climb it after all.

Next, we went to the Kawaguchiko Natural Living Centre. There we observed the heavily manicured gardens full of lavender and roses. We signed up for a fruit picking session as soon as we arrived. Luckily they had a couple of seats available. We spent roughly forty minutes picking cherries and blueberries, and we ate them for our lunch. Beth thought it would be fun to race and see who could pick the most; she won. The woman had wizard fingers.

I'd never been a huge lover of museums, so when Beth suggested the Kubota Itchiku Art Museum I sighed, but she assured me I'd love it. When we got there the archway entrance looked like something out of an Indiana Jones movie, and my interest skyrocketed. As a kid, I'd always wanted to explore ancient ruins and have my own *Goonies* adventure with my friends, but maybe without the dead body in the freezer.

The art didn't intrigue me too much, but there was a gorgeous waterfall and several places to kick back and relax. There was a tearoom on the second floor with a view of a small pond and pretty overgrown trees. We took the time to hydrate whilst taking cover from the sun.

On our way out of the museum we were told to walk through the maple corridor. It was a short path, maybe fifty metres in length, flanked on either side by maple trees—hence the name. The guide at the museum informed us it was best to visit in the fall, but there was an adequate breeze today that would allow us to get a smell of the sweet aroma.

"I'm tempted to bite the bark off that tree," I joked.

"Don't do that." Beth laughed.

"It smells incredible though, doesn't it?" We turned our noses into the wind like dogs trying to find a scent.

"Amazing!"

We took the bus down to the lakeside and strolled along the lake's edge. We walked through canopied walkways, climbing up and up, until we reached Ubuyagasaki Cape, where we witnessed another spectacular view of Mount Fuji. Across the bridge and down by the lake's shore we stopped at a small cafe for a coffee and some chocolate cake.

"Thank you for today," I said.

"You've enjoyed it then?"

"I have loved every minute." It wasn't a complete distraction, as I checked my phone for the fiftieth time that day. No reply. I knew Brooke was working, but I felt sad when I didn't see her name on my screen.

"Have you decided what you're going to do tomorrow?" Beth asked.

We hadn't decided when she'd asked me that morning, and due to Brooke's lack of contact there was still no definitive answer.

"Nope." I shrugged. "I'm thinking food though, something that just involves eating and drinking all day," I said as I devoured my chocolate cake.

"Good idea. Tsukiji Market would be a great place to start. Me and Ren used to go a lot when we lived closer to the centre. Oh my god, they do the best omelette, but you do have to get there early to avoid queues."

Beth placed her hand to her mouth. "I feel . . ." She retched. "I don't think eggs will be a favourite of mine throughout this pregnancy." Beth grabbed her coffee.

She'd almost thrown up the night before when I devoured some sushi in front of her.

"Okay, so no omelette for you then."

"I'm not exactly selling this to you. Wait, I have a picture on my feed somewhere." She searched her phone, and within seconds flashed a picture of what looked like a slab of butter in a tray, but apparently it was egg.

"It looks . . . different."

"Trust me, just try some."

I was grateful for whatever distraction Beth could provide, and if that involved slabs of egg and retching, then so be it.

The anticipation I felt for the following day was so much more than I'd hoped to feel. Why couldn't I just be emotionless and void of love towards Brooke? It might be a bland and sad existence, but at least my heart would remain intact and my whole body wouldn't continuously cry out for someone it couldn't have.

I wasn't stupid. I liked to think my career success proved that, but what was my best-case scenario? Sleep with Brooke once every couple of years when I came to Japan until one of us fell in love with someone else? Then that would be off the cards too; then what? She'd become someone I used to know, an anecdote about the time I had my heart broken.

*

When we returned home later that night my feet were swollen from all the walking. My calves felt tight. My body was clammy and exhausted. I ran for a refreshing shower and collapsed on the sofa.

"Do you want some of your Alfort biscuits?" Beth called from the kitchen.

"Yes please." The idea of the vanilla flavoured white chocolate made my mouth water.

"Here you go." She lobbed them over the back of the sofa.

"What have you got?" I asked.

Beth lowered her plate as she walked past, so I could see the four colourful mochi desserts.

"I love them! They've started doing them everywhere in London. They're so good."

"I didn't understand them at first, especially this little passion fruit one. Don't you think it looks like a ball sack?" Beth picked up the mochi ball and started squeezing it.

"A ball sack?" I burst out laughing. "I can't say men's genitals often come into my description of anything, but now you say it." It was a strange wrinkly texture with a skin-coloured complexion.

"What's the greeny coloured one?"

"Mint chocolate chip, it's my new favourite," Beth replied.

My phone started vibrating excessively. One message came in after another to the point where the sofa felt like a massage chair; it was Paula.

Paula
Got a new case.

Paula
High-profile murder in Kensington.

Paula
Defendant specifically requested you to represent them.

Paula
Serious media coverage. He can pay the big bucks.

Her message was followed by numerous bags of money emojis. When Paula was excited, she couldn't type one long message; she had to do it in small parts.

Paula
Look at the BBC News app.

I opened the app. The first news story read—*Millionaire businessman accused of murdering his ex-wife's new boyfriend*—It pricked my interest instantly.

Holly
Interesting. Why does he want me?

Requests for my representation increased the longer my winning streak prevailed. A high-profile case meant exposure, which meant higher fees and unlimited resources.

Paula
I have no idea. It's not like you're any good at your job.

Paula added three laughing emojis.

Holly
Funny. Will you set up a meeting with him and gather all the relevant information ASAP? I can review the case as soon as I receive it and set up an appointment after that.

I liked to move quick. Clients didn't have time to wait.

Paula
Already done. I'm speaking with him at noon today.

I noted the time, it must've been 5 a.m. in London.

Holly
Perfect. Early riser today? Did you piss yourself?

In my absence she had no choice but to get up early, and I know she hated me for it.

Paula
Yes, you do that with old age. That, and the lawyer I work with has taken herself halfway across the world and I'm left to deal with her shit.

A poop shaped emoji followed.

Holly
She sounds terrible.

I joked.

Paula
She is. Are you coming back yet? Getting up pre-6 a.m. is not good for me. I looked haggard before, but my eyes now resemble two hollow caves.

The message came with a photo attachment of Paula half asleep sat at her breakfast bar with a cup of coffee and her famous red hair poking out in every direction.

Holly
You look delicious. Only seven days to go and you'll have me back.

I spent the next ten minutes reading through some articles about my potential new case. There was always a buzz when someone requested me personally, especially for such a high-profile case. I didn't enjoy dealing with the media frenzy that accompanied such serious accusations, but any lawyer would agree it was part of the package.

"What are you smiling at?" Beth asked.

"New case."

"Huh." She fell silent.

"What?"

"I thought it might've been Brooke with the way you've been smirking at your phone."

"No, just Paula being Paula." I smiled. I wished it was Brooke.

Beth returned her eyes to the TV. She was watching some Japanese show I couldn't follow. I'm not sure she could either, but she laughed every so often suggesting she understood the comedy.

Brooke should've finished work an hour ago, but she'd made no contact.

"Will you keep your foot still." Beth grabbed my toes from the other end of the sofa and squeezed.

"Ouch! I can't help that I'm fidgety."

"No, you're not normally, but you've been moving your feet back and forth since we sat down. Just text the girl if it's making you nervous."

"How do you know she hasn't already texted me?"

"Because I know you, and I can tell you're distracted. You have been all day." She said matter-of-factly.

"I'm sorry. I don't mean to seem distracted."

Beth blinked. "I know."

"Are you okay with me going with Brooke tomorrow? I obviously came here to spend time with you. I wouldn't want you to think I don't want to do that."

"Am I okay? I'm delighted. No offence." She paused. "You know I love you, but I'm exhausted, and I am more than happy to just relax at home."

"Way to make a girl feel welcome," I joked.

"Shut up." She bent my toe until I squealed. "Ow!" I whacked her hand away, and we proceeded to wrestle with each other's legs until my phone broke up the brawl. It was Brooke calling. Finally.

"I'm going to take this in my room."

"Okay loser."

I ran into the bedroom, composing myself before I clicked the green button.

"Hey." I leaned back against the chest of drawers. I felt casual and cool, but it's not like she could see me.

"Hi, sorry I didn't text you back earlier. I've been super busy."

"Don't worry, I wasn't waiting around desperately for your reply," I jested. I definitely was. "How was work?"

"Good. Busy. The usual. Why don't you tell me about your day? What parts of Japan have you explored today?"

I got the feeling she didn't want to talk about work. That didn't bother me; maybe she'd had a stressful day. I reeled off the places me and Beth had been and my favourite parts. She asked questions about each of them; some she'd seen herself, others not, but she showed a real interest. I loved that.

"That all sounds amazing." I sensed something was off. Her tone was strained. She didn't seem upbeat.

"Is everything okay with you?" I asked.

"Of course, why wouldn't it be?"

I paced back and forth; standing still was almost impossible when I was on the phone. "I don't know, you just sound a little down."

"I'm fine, Holly. It's just been a crazy day. I promise I won't be miserable tomorrow. Speaking of tomorrow, what are we doing?" Subject changed. She was getting rather good at that.

"I was going to ask you the same thing. I like the idea of a foodie day. I'd love to experiment with more Japanese cuisine." My stomach rumbled as soon as I mentioned food; having filled up on sweet stuff all day I was yet to have a proper meal.

"Okay, we can do that. I can have a think tonight. I'll text a couple of my friends from work and pull a little itinerary together for us."

"I like the sound of that."

"What time shall we meet?"

"Beth mentioned a market in the city where they do this amazing omelette for breakfast. Apparently getting there early is essential."

"Tsukiji Market?" Brooke asked.

"That sounds like it, yes."

"I know exactly what omelette she means. I agree. You have to try it."

"How do you want to meet?"

"I think it'll be easier if we get the train. Do you want to meet me at the station? There's one right by the market. It's in Chuo. I can send over which train you need to catch once we get off the phone."

"Okay."

"Does 8 a.m. work for you?" Brooke asked.

The early start didn't concern me; the more time I got to spend with her the better.

"Sounds perfect."

The phone call didn't end there. I lay on my bed like a teenager, twiddling my hair and catching up with my crush, as I would've been in high school. I just needed to be chewing gum and watching reruns of *The O.C.*

We caught up on some work gossip. She was shocked to hear that Mr. West had divorced and was now dating a forty-year-old fashion magazine editor.

"He's sixty-three!"

"I know!"

"Do you think she's in it for the money?"

"I think she's got her own money. He is quite handsome for his age though, a bit like a Brad Pitt mixed with Jim Carrey."

"That's the oddest combination I've ever heard." Brooke laughed.

We spoke at length about what she did in her free time, which was noticeably more interesting than what I did. She played golf; that was new. She liked to sing at a karaoke bar every other Friday, also new. I'd never heard her sing.

"I promise you, I'm not good, but my friends from work love to sing, so I kind of just joined in."

"What's your go to karaoke song?"

"If you can guess I'll buy you lunch tomorrow," Brooke challenged.

I'd gotten a flavour of her playlist on our drive to the national park. It was similar to my own. Would she go for a classic upbeat song or a ballad?

"Hmm . . . I have two."

"Okay." I could sense her smiling.

"I think if you want to have a bit of fun with it and get others singing along, you go for 'A Thousand Miles' by Vanessa Carlton." It was an obvious choice. It was a karaoke classic and a staple song in a film we both loved—*White Chicks*. She didn't say a word.

"Now, if you want to show off your vocal skills, which you say you haven't got, or just sing a song you love, I think you'd go for 'California King Bed' by Rihanna."

The phone line was so quiet I could hear the faint sounds of music in the background.

"Brooke? Are you still there?"

"How . . . How do you do that?"

I could hear "P.S. (I'm Still Not Over You)" playing in the background. She'd always been a huge Rihanna fan.

"Was I right?" I beamed.

"Yes, but I have been mixing it up a bit lately. Of all the Rihanna songs, why that one?"

"Lucky guess," I lied.

It wasn't a lucky guess at all. I had many fond memories with Brooke, despite our short time together and the whole period being clouded by the not so fond memories. I recalled spending the night at her house like it was yesterday. Brooke chose an appropriate playlist to match our mood—it happened to be Rihanna. After the initial sex, I lay beside her watching her mouth every word to "California King Bed". It seemed like such an insignificant moment at the time, but I knew then she would have an impact on my life so great I would never forget her.

When it came to asking about what I did now, it was depressingly straight forward; I worked.

She asked me about my thirtieth birthday. I didn't tell her I'd been disappointed not to hear from her. I made out as though it was amazing, and skimmed over the minor details, like how my mum almost threw out the thing I cherished most in the world, and of course Francesca.

I had refrained from bringing up any relationships or dating history from the past two years, and so had she. It was the last thing I wanted to know. I would rather be naive to the facts. The thought of her being with someone else made me sick to my core.

We tried to fill in the missing pieces from the past two years without broaching the subject of how we left things or how things were currently playing out. There was a pause every so often in the middle of a story where I would think and redirect. Many of those stories involved Francesca. I didn't want to cause any unnecessary pain, but I wouldn't lie to her if she asked me outright. She did the exact same pause. She chose her words carefully whenever she spoke about her life, almost like she was hiding something.

It was part of my job to read people. It was harder to do over the phone, but I could sense when someone was refraining from telling me the whole truth. Brooke offered few details about her life, and she often repeated the question before answering it, both were tell-tale signs she was avoiding telling me something, but what?

I wasn't sure I wanted to know.

CHAPTER ELEVEN

Beth's kitchen was dark, but I'd heard a clatter; it sounded like a pan, so I figured it was best to go and investigate.

Why does it sound like something is sizz—

"How did you sleep?" Beth whispered.

"Shit, Beth." I recoiled. "You nearly gave me a heart attack."

She grinned back. The blinds were drawn with no lights on, and she was stood quietly frying some bananas over the stove.

"I've been up since 5 a.m. Surely you heard me?"

"Nope. You're like a ninja. What are you cooking?" I sniffed. The smell surrounded me as I got closer. The sweet scent filled my lungs. I recognised the smell—it was a red flag.

"Banana muffins," Beth said, chewing on the inside of her cheek. She'd done that since I'd known her, but usually it meant she was harbouring a secret.

"Why?" I rubbed at my eyes.

"Because I've been craving caramelised banana all night, and I could barely sleep." She poured some more sugar in the pan.

"Caramelised banana muffins? They sound amazing."

"Yes, with Nutella." She winked.

"Wow."

"I know. I'm not just saying this because I make them, but they're to die for."

"I bet."

Beth added the caramelised banana to the batter before adding an excessive amount of Nutella.

"You like banana muffins, right?"

"That's like asking a child if they like McDonald's." I walked around the kitchen counter and stuck my finger in the mixture.

"Hey." She tapped me with the batter covered spoon causing it to splatter all up my arm. "More for me." I stuck my tongue out.

"I don't know where those fingers of yours have been . . . Scratch that. I do know, and I don't want them in my muffins." The whole sentence was a sexual inuendo waiting to happen; I couldn't resist.

"I know, believe me, I've tried," I joked.

"You're disgusting." She proceeded to separate the mixture into the muffin tins with precise measurements.

She was stalling.

I could sense something was off.

"What time did you say Brooke was working yesterday?" She was terrible at being discreet, always had been. It was a random question.

"Erm, her shift was 11-8, I believe."

"Huh." Beth placed the muffins in the oven.

"What?"

"Well . . ." She hesitated. I hated it when she started any sentence with, well—

"Ren went to Chaos Kitchen for some food yesterday evening. He does that when he's working in the city. I told him to look out for Brooke. He can be nosey like a woman sometimes. I think that's why I love him. He's been dying to see who the mysterious Brooke is." She flicked the towel over her shoulder and proceeded to wipe the kitchen sides down with a cloth. She wouldn't look me in the eye.

"Jesus Christ. Please tell me he didn't do anything embarrassing."

"No . . . This is the thing; she wasn't there." Beth turned and raised her eyebrow.

"Oh, maybe she was on her break?" That was a logical explanation, right?

"That's what I thought, but after he'd finished eating, he went to grab a drink from Sake Bar. He overhead one of the waiters talking to a customer and apologising for the delay. He said they were short staffed. There was only him and some other guy behind the bar working that evening." Beth looked like she wanted to disappear into the leftover mixture.

"Oh." I focused on the worktop where the splatters of batter left a trail to the sink.

"Yeah, I didn't know whether to say anything. I just thought you should know."

"Is that why you're up so early?" I asked.

"Kind of. I mulled it over all night, decided not to tell you, then to tell you, and it went like that for a few hours."

"I'd be mad if you didn't tell me."

"I know." Beth boiled the kettle and reached for two mugs from the fancy metal wall display she'd created. "Listen, regardless of whatever it is you're doing whilst you're here in Japan, how significant it is or not, you should know if you're being lied to."

"Why would she lie to me?"

"Your guess is as good as mine." Beth shrugged.

Is she lying to me?

Does it matter if she is?

It would sting, but nothing could sting as much as the day she left.

"What shall I do?"

"If she's lied to you, it's probably for a good reason. I wouldn't dwell on it too much. Whatever the two of you are doing, you'll be gone in six days, so it seems pointless to challenge her." Beth made a good point.

"You're right," I tried to reassure myself. "She seemed pretty embarrassed and defensive about my thoughts on her father the other day, so it's probably something to do with him. No doubt he's still ruling her life like she's a teenager."

"Probably. I'm glad my dad's not like that."

"Ditto."

Brooke's business was none of mine, not really. Whatever ties we had to one another ended two years ago, even if the feelings were still present, even if they were stronger than ever. What we had was history. She didn't owe me anything.

I had to forget about it and enjoy the time I had left with her before it was over—again.

*

The train line was heaving. Thankfully, Beth waited with me until the train arrived on the platform. The temperature outside was twenty-four degrees already, and it was only 7:30 a.m. I had a string of ten text messages from Paula, all regarding work, until the very last one caught my attention.

Paula
Have you bumped into Brooke yet?

A monkey face emoji followed. I'd left that part out of our conversations and for good reason. The main one being me not wanting her opinion.

Holly
Beth told you, didn't she?

Beth and Paula decided, after meeting a grand total of three times and bonding over thinking I'd been eaten by a black bear that they were now best buddies, and the joint CEOs of my love life.

Paula
Yes, she may have told me. When you don't reply to me, I now ask Beth.

Fantastic.

Holly
You're nosey. Don't go telling anyone!

I found a comfortable forward-facing seat on the train, because I can't travel backwards.

Paula
I wouldn't dream of it. Especially not Ashleigh. I still have high hopes for you and Francesca. I don't want to see that perish because of your ludicrous holiday romance.

Paula was the champion of a future Francesca and Holly romance.
The journey was pleasant. The air-con on board was state of the art, so I forgot how hot it was until I stepped

off the train thirty minutes later. I exited into a crowd of people, like cattle being herded off the platform. I moved with the majority until I came to a safe chaos free zone over by the ticket stand.

I felt a tap on my shoulder.

"Hey," I yelled, as I pulled my earbuds out.

"Hi." Brooke grinned. "I waved at you from the stairs over there, but I think you were too busy trying not to get trampled." She smirked.

I hesitated to hug her, and so did she. I motioned forward, and she followed. The embrace felt awkward and uncertain. How do you greet someone you used to be in love with? Are *still* in love with? After having passionate sex in the back of a car? I suspected there wasn't a one-size-fits-all answer.

Brooke's appearance took me back to our previous train platform encounter in the London underground. She wore a khaki dress, but it was less formal this time. The jersey material was fit for a summer's day. It was low-cut around the neck, sleeveless, tight around her hips, and holding her figure like a glove. Her long blonde hair was down and wavy. When I saw her at Nina's coffee shop before she moved to Japan, she'd added some brown. That had fully disappeared now.

"It's worse than London." That is something I never thought I'd say.

"I know. It can get hectic." She glanced at my outfit. I felt self-conscious. I had on a pair of New Balance trainers. They were much more comfortable than the Converse. I wore a pair of baggy denim jeans and a cropped vintage varsity style T-shirt. I felt attractive. I'd made the effort to wash my hair and curl my eyelashes. I didn't want to apply any makeup because I was positive the sun would melt it off. Beth had been kind enough to lend me a Japanese fake tan mist, which happened to be one of the best on the market, no smell, no streaks, and a healthy glow.

"You look really good. I like what you're wearing." Brooke said.

I sighed with relief.

"Thank you. I was about to say the same to you," I replied.

My eyes rested on her lips for a moment. I'd kissed those lips two days ago, but the possibility now seemed terrifying.

"Shall we?" Brooke took the lead, and my nostrils were suddenly filled with a scent so unbelievably perfect that if I could've bottled it up, I would have. It was musky, with maybe a jasmine base.

I fell behind as Brooke rushed out onto the streets of Tsukiji. She eventually linked arms with me; clearly my slow pace was a hinderance. When we reached Tsukiji Market it was bustling with locals and tourists alike. Brooke led me towards a food stand with a giant green and yellow sign. I had no idea what it said, but I saw a queue of at least twenty people waiting for the little white tray. Each person dispersed carrying the large slab of omelette like it was precious cargo.

"This is the place?" I asked.

"The best *tamagoyaki* in town." Brooke grinned.

"Is that what it's called? I wonder what makes this one so good."

"It's the sweetness. I don't know what they put in it, maybe sugar, but it's so nice. It has this like custardy texture, which might sound disgusting right now, but wait until you've tried it."

The queue went down within minutes. There were three different chefs baking and cutting the *tamagoyaki* with impressive speed. We got ours and sat to the left on a row of benches for *paying customers only*, as the sign stated in both Japanese and English.

Brooke observed me curiously as I sliced the first section. It was fresh from the pan, so the heat required a few dramatic blows to cool it down. My mouth watered, and my taste buds went wild: the sweetness, the texture, the way it crumbled in my mouth; the taste was magnificent.

"Well?" Brooke said.

"Mmm."

"Good?"

I nodded as I took another bite.

"It certainly beats my omelettes." An omelette was my go-to single person dinner because it was easy. I would fry some mushrooms, onions, and peppers in a pan, add two eggs, salt and pepper, and a handful of cheese. It was a breakfast, dinner, or tea kind of meal. Well, it was for me. "Mind the pun."

"Whenever I try to make an omelette, I always overcook it. It falls to pieces on my plate, and it looks disgusting," Brooke added.

"You can't be good at everything." I smirked.

"You are." She rolled her eyes.

"I am not."

"Name one thing you're not good at." Brooke said between mouthfuls.

"Fixing cars." I would love to be able to fix cars; it seemed like such an investment.

"One thing that isn't a profession you have to spend years training in," Brooke hit back.

"Easy. I can't play tennis."

"Really? Tennis?"

I'd had a hard time figuring out how to swing the racket without it flying out of my hand at high speed, or swinging completely off balance and whacking my shin instead of the ball. It was not an easy sport. I credited the professionals.

"What? I was obsessed with Serena Williams when I was a kid. I watched the Grand Slams religiously with my dad. I even asked my mum for a tennis outfit for Christmas one year. I tried to play, but it wasn't for me, anyone could've beaten me blindfolded with one hand tied behind their back." I said.

"Huh. You told me you were great at badminton as a kid? How are you good at that but terrible at tennis? They're basically the same thing," Brooke said suspiciously.

"Go figure." I shrugged. "Not sure they are though. One requires grace, a light touch, and lightening reflexes; the other requires the power of an ox and a grunt that would put a Russian porn star to shame."

Was it only me who found it uncomfortable watching women and men grunt and sweat with my parents in the same room?

"Where you bad because you were expecting to be Serena Williams?"

I devoured the last mouthful of *tamagoyaki*. I would certainly be coming back for another before the end of my trip.

"Maybe." I laughed.

"Okay, did you ever win a tournament playing tennis?"

"Once, I think." The other player was worse than I was. I didn't think it was possible. Turns out there were other kids who were also bad at tennis.

"I knew it! You have to give me something else." We stood and dropped our trays in the bin.

"Okay, I don't know . . . Dating." I chuckled.

"I beg to differ."

"My recent dating history has been bleak." I nudged her slightly; it was intended as a joke, but her gaze hit the floor and she didn't respond. "I'm joking."

The pavement was so narrow and densely packed with people that when Brooke dodged an oncoming pedestrian, she slipped off the edge and narrowly missed the large fluorescent orange cones cordoning off the road.

"Shit!" she yelled. I grabbed her arm. My lightening reflexes from my badminton days were paying off.

"Careful." I chuckled.

"Shall we walk around the outside?"

"I think that's a good idea."

We went into the centre of the street where there was more wiggle room. A man stood waving a large green flag and shouting, "bluefin tuna." I thought about it, but Brooke's strong walk past the short bearded man reminded me she was vegetarian.

"So . . ." Brooke slid her body sideways past a woman with a suitcase and a man with several large bin bags. I felt like we were in an old school Nintendo game where you had to duck, dive, and weave your way around obstacles.

"So what?" I smiled.

"With you saying recent dating history—" A man on a white moped sped through the middle of everyone. He pulled up with a screech outside a food stall with a giant eel and skewers of meat on the sign.

Eww.

"I'm kind of curious," she finished.

"Okay," I said. The latter part of the word was drawn out.

"Have you been dating anyone?" Brooke said. The words came out in a flurry. Her cheeks flushed.

She glanced at the eel skewers and pulled a disgusted face, which left me bemused. Between narrowly missing the plethora of accidents waiting to happen, she looked up and I think she caught me smirking.

Scrap that. She 100 percent caught me smirking.

"I'll take that as a yes." Brooke laughed.

"No, I'm not smirking because of your question. I just think it's funny we're trying to have a serious conversation whilst dodging bodies. I feel like I'm on an episode of *Takeshi's Castle*," I said.

Brooke did a cute half laugh half-smile. Back in London I fell in love with that half laugh, the curl of her lips, the crinkle of her eyes, and the elevation of her cheeks that created the tiny laugh lines around her mouth. Perfection.

"What?" Brooke asked.

"Nothing."

"You're staring at me."

Was it that obvious?

"Sorry." I looked to the right and my eyes were drawn to a shop on the corner covered in strawberry decor. I stopped dead in my tracks. "I want whatever they're selling."

Brooke linked our arms and pushed me towards the queue. "I thought you might."

It seems I had escaped the dating question for now.

The display case was full of different confectionary items with strawberries incorporated. It was heaven, if you liked strawberries, which I did. The final choice was between custard-filled mochi with a strawberry on top, strawberry skewers covered in what looked like syrup, or a strawberry swirl ice cream in a wafer cone, also with a strawberry on top.

The latter looked like the most popular, but the least edible. It looked fake, like it should be in *Charlie and the Chocolate Factory,* or like the fake food you find on a food counter in Spain, to show you how nice the food could look, but it never quite does.

"Does that look fake to you?" I nodded towards the ice cream.

"I think that one is for show purposes, otherwise it'd be melting," Brooke said sarcastically.

"I know *that* one is, I just mean in general. Look, that girl just ordered one. Let me watch her lick it." I bobbed my head to get a good look.

"Okay, weirdo. Let's just get one and test it." She pulled me forward.

At the front counter, the lady serving us offered a sample of the custard mochi that determined beyond reasonable doubt that it was the nicest thing I'd tasted in my life. I bought eight.

It was greedy. I was aware, but I wasn't about to eat them all at once. I would share with Beth.

"Are you going to tell me who you've been dating?" asked Brooke.

Gulp. She wasn't letting it go.

"Erm." I laughed nervously.

"Or do I have to steal your phone, unblock me on your social media, and stalk your most recent pictures to see who liked them?" Brooke raised her eyebrow suspiciously.

"Very specific."

I wasn't sure if she was hoping I'd say no, or if she was genuinely curious to know who her predecessor was.

I tried to broach the subject as carefully as I could. There was no use in me lying.

"There was one woman." Brooke's eyes narrowed; her expression was pinched. "Her name is Francesca."

"Oh." She paused. "That's a pretty name."

"She's Italian."

Why did you say that?

If I could've hit myself in the face, I would've.

What did her ethnicity have to do with anything?

"And is Francesca still in the picture?" She wouldn't look me in the eye, but she knew the answer.

"Of course not. I wouldn't have. We wouldn't have, y'know."

"Had sex?" Brooke asked.

"Exactly."

Or at least I'd like to think not, but it was Brooke, and anything was possible, including infidelity. Thankfully, I hadn't been put in that position. There was a strange look on her face. It looked like guilt.

"What happened? How did you start dating?"

"Do you really want to know?" I asked.

"Yes," she said confidently.

There was the truth and the real truth. The watered-down version or the emotional debacle that resulted in my untimely end with dating in general. We strolled through the inside of the market. The atmosphere felt wrong for the conversation, but it did help ease the tension. It beat having the conversation over a dinner table with little background noise and nowhere else to look.

"I don't know if you ever met my friend Jake; he works the bar scene in London. One night he asked if he could set me up on a blind date."

Brooke's eyes widened in amusement.

"A blind date, huh?"

"Yes, my thoughts exactly. I wasn't looking forward to it. I was expecting this whole uncomfortable ordeal where I'd want to leave immediately, but I wanted to get him off my back, so I agreed."

From the inside of the market, we headed across the road until we hit a side street. A few doors down we found a coffee shop.

"I was ten minutes late because of traffic. When I arrived I thought she'd left. I couldn't see anyone single, so I went to the toilet, and there was a woman on the phone. She was speaking Italian. I had no idea what she was saying. We both sort of looked at each other in the mirror; I smiled politely. I thought she was beautiful, but no way did I think she was my blind date."

I opened the door to enter the coffee shop.

"Turns out she was my blind date."

We paused the conversation to order two iced lattes. There was a vacant red bench outside the coffee shop, so we took a seat.

"Did you hit it off?" Brooke asked.

"Erm, yes. Not instantly. It wasn't like sparks flying or anything, but she was a nice girl. I liked her energy." I removed the square sunglasses I'd purchased from the airport; we were covered by shade now.

"Where you together long?"

"Only a few months. It wasn't serious; it didn't get to that stage." That was my fault, I thought. Paula often reminded me I would live to regret it.

"What happened?"

She asked every question with reluctance in her voice. I could tell she didn't want to know, but she did, if that makes sense. Maybe she wanted some clarity like

I did. Maybe it would make her feel less guilty about leaving things the way she had.

Did she want to hear I'd moved on with someone else to feel less burdened by it all? It was possible.

"I guess she realised I wasn't emotionally available. Apparently that's kind of a deal breaker." I wasn't about to get into the birthday party letter scenario.

"Oh." Brooke took another long sip of her latte. "But you liked her?"

"Sure." I looked up at the clear blue sky.

"That's the kind of response you give when you get asked if you enjoyed watching a movie at the cinema." She laughed.

"I don't know what else you want me to say." I shrugged.

"Is she funny? Is she adventurous? Could you see yourself together one day? Is she kind? Does she like sports? Fashion?"

"Why are you pushing me?" I asked.

"I'm not. I just want to know what she's like."

"Well, she's all of those things, I guess."

Brooke rolled her eyes at my lack of response.

"How about what she isn't then?"

I couldn't understand why she was fishing so hard for answers, and I was battling with just how honest I should be. Rather than beat around the bush, I said the first thing that came to mind, and it was the whole truth.

"She's not *you*."

CHAPTER TWELVE

How do you know if you truly love someone?

There were a few tell-tale signs I immediately thought of. You think about them constantly, want to spend as much time with them as possible, and you don't see a future without them in it. You smile awkwardly for no reason; you laugh uncontrollably at things that aren't funny. You become a happier person. I know what that feels like. I felt it in my first relationship with Danielle, and I felt it with Brooke.

Loving someone you can't have was a whole different ball game. It was like taking a case and finding out the client I've been hired to defend was guilty. My job was to win the case, despite the odds and my opinions. It was tough, sometimes soul destroying, but it was my job. It was the career I'd chosen, and like anything, there came good with the bad, and I could change it if I chose to do so. I could opt out, find another job, retrain, and push myself to succeed in another field.

It was similar to relationships, I guess. When things didn't work out, we mourned the loss, and then we moved on. We tried again, learned from our previous relationships, and tried to succeed the next time.

Problems arose from unnatural endings. When two people were torn apart through outside influences, tragedy, or misconception, things could get complicated. I once had a client who'd lost his wife. She was only twenty-nine years old. It was a tragic car accident caused by a drunk driver. I remembered that case vividly. I remembered asking him what the loss meant to him, and how it affected his life. Those may seem like stupid questions with obvious answers, but how he answered stuck with me. He didn't say, *I'm heartbroken, I miss her*, or *Life isn't the same without her*. All valid things to say, and more than likely true; instead, what he said struck me to my core.

"I will never be able to breathe the same again. I'm numb now physically and mentally. I wander through life with little knowledge of what is happening around me. I feel sorry for my family, my friends, and the future partner I may one day have. The day my wife died my life changed forever. I will never enjoy life the way I did for the first thirty years. I still laugh and smile, but there's a deep sadness in place of what once was happiness, a sadness that exudes from my body like blood oozing from my veins. It's constant, and that's my reality now, but I have no regrets. I found my soulmate, and I will be eternally grateful."

The words brought tears to my eyes back then, but what I remember most was the uninhabited look on his face. The soft smile he put on to try and deceive everyone around him. The blank stare that flickered from left to right. He couldn't hold eye contact for fear I'd see the pain behind his eyes.

Brooke was doing the same thing. After my off the cuff but truthful comment she excused herself to go to the ladies' room. Five minutes later she hadn't returned. I thought about the stereotypical first date scenario where the person climbs out the bathroom window and never returns. The chime of the door sounded and out walked Brooke.

"I thought you'd ditched me," I joked.

"Of course not. I was asking the owner how they make that coffee; it was incredible." Her eyes looked red, she'd been crying, but I didn't make it obvious I noticed.

"Where to next?" I asked.

She linked arms with me. "We need to head back to Tsukiji Station. We're going to a place that does the best melon pan."

Just like that, we both ignored the hurt once again, and chose to move on with the day.

We took the train to Ginza. On route Brooke explained melon pan. It was essentially bread with a sugary crust, and it was filled with melon flavoured cream. I pictured a doughnut, but she assured me it was way better.

"You know a lot, considering you've only been here two years. You're a good tour guide."

She shrugged. "I tried to explore as much as I could when I first got here. I had a lot of free time. I spent weeks riding around on the trains and figuring it out. Then, when I met Takara . . . Well, she showed me a lot too."

There was that awkward look again, I noted it.

"Must be nice to have a close friend like that. She's like your guide to all things Japan."

"Yeah, it's great." Brooke turned towards the window. She reached out and gripped my hand, tighter than necessary, like she was afraid I'd let go.

"Holly . . ." The train came to a slow halt, and the announcer indicated this was the stop for Ginza. We gathered our things and exited the platform promptly.

"Did you want to say something?" I asked.

"What? When?"

"Just then, on the train, it seemed like you were about to say something."

"No . . . I was erm . . . just going to say something soppy and embarrassing. I'll save it for later."

She grabbed my hand and intertwined her fingers with mine. My heart swelled with pride. Our reunion would be fleeting, but in that moment, I was incredibly proud to have her by my side once again, however short lived our time might be.

"I'll hold you to that."

She seemed hesitant. I wasn't sure if it was nerves or something more, but I tried to ignore it. I thought about asking her if she'd been dating anyone since me; she knew about Francesca, so it seemed appropriate, but the thought put me off our next food stop, so I didn't. As the saying goes; what you don't know doesn't hurt you.

Inside the glass front building was a counter full of wooden boxes filled with baked goods. We'd come for the melon pan, but I couldn't resist the rest.

"I'd like some of that apple pie as well. Oh my God, what is that?" It looked like a box full of the fluffiest bread I'd ever seen.

"Kashi pan. It's bread with filling," Brooke said.

"Oh wow, they do cream cheese . . . and strawberry . . . I want both." I was in my element, hypnotised by the sweet smell of pastry. I left with a bag full.

"Shall we try it?" I asked.

Brooked nodded.

I pulled the melon pan from the bag; it was still slightly warm, which indicated just how fresh it was. The melon cream began to seep into my mouth. The flavour overwhelmed my taste buds in the best way. The mixture of soft warm bread and sweet sugary cream was incomparable to anything else, even a Krispy Kreme doughnut, and they were my favourite.

"Good?" Brooke chuckled.

"Mmmhmm. Unreal." She went to grab the bread from my hands, but she was too slow. "All mine." I winked.

"Oh, come on!" She reached again, but I had the height advantage, so I held the delicious pastry above my head.

"I hope the melon drops in your hair," Brooke said before turning and walking off.

I ran to catch up with her, almost falling off the curb laughing. "Okay, okay . . . Here you go."

Brooke turned with a smug look on her face. I reached forwards to offer her a bite, and the opportunity to be naughty presented itself. I lightly pressed the bread against her nose; it was just enough to leave a dollop of melon cream on the tip.

"Oh, I see. That's how you want to play," Brooke said with a mischievous smile. She wiped the cream from her nose and lunged forward. I jumped backwards and ran across the street at speed, narrowly missing a lamppost and a stationary car. I raced down a side street, dodging pedestrians, crates of produce, and bikes until I hit a dead end. I had nowhere to go. Brooke was closing in.

"Woah. Okay. We can negotiate. Let's work out a deal." I held my hands up in surrender.

"Just, no melon in my hair. Please." I pleaded.

She gently teased, edging forwards little by little. My eyes glued to the dollop of sticky cream on her fingertips.

Brooke pushed me up against the white brick wall of an unknown department store. The only audience was the naked window mannequins stood by the dumpster and the occasional worker running from the back entrance to the bins. It was far from picturesque, but the atmosphere didn't matter. Our connection prevailed as it always did.

I held my breath as Brooke moved in closer. I think I stopped breathing for a few seconds.

"Hi," I said softly, keeping one eye on the fingers holding the melon cream. Brooke smirked and licked the cream from her fingers. I don't think it was intended to be sexual. The scenario was far from it, but she could be sat in a dumpster reading a dictionary, and I'd find it sexy.

She stepped forward, moving her leg between mine. Her hand brushed the length of my arm. I didn't move. I let her take the lead. She traced my bottom lip with the tip of her index finger, leaned forward, and took my bottom lip in her teeth tugging gently. The sensation took me completely by surprise.

When she looked into my eyes, she didn't hesitate. I could tell she felt the same desire I did. Before I could question whether it was the right thing to do, her mouth was on mine. I placed my hand on the back of her neck, pulling her in closer. Her lips parted. She allowed me to explore the inside of her mouth. The sweet melon taste only made me want her more.

The moment was sure to get out of hand, but—

"I think we're being watched," I said. Brooke released my mouth from her captivity and turned to observe a small woman stood in her green apron. She wasn't being discreet. She clearly disapproved of two women using the alleyway behind her restaurant as a place to pack on the PDA.

Brooke laughed and pulled me away. "She got more than she bargained for."

"I think we both did."

"Hmm, and it's only 11 a.m." Brooke grinned.

We'd been together for over two hours. She saw that as a good thing. I saw it as the opposite. We were being followed by a giant ticking clock. It was haunting me, and I didn't know how to make it stop.

"Where to next?" I didn't care, preferably anywhere that would slow the time down.

"There's a department store around the corner. They do this amazing dish; I can't remember what it's called. Hold on, let me ask my friend from work." She typed away on her phone. About a minute later it buzzed back.

"That's it, *Tsukimi Tsukune*."

"What's that?" I asked.

"Japan's answer to a Scotch egg."

I was intrigued.

We crossed the road and entered the large department store. It looked like a Japanese version of Selfridges. We passed through the cosmetics department and took the elevator to the food hall. We wandered each section until we came across a row of glass cabinets filled with savoury produce.

They had everything from skewered meat to prawns and raw sushi. Brooke pointed to a tray of golf ball sized fried goods. They appeared to be glazed in something and greasy, not normally my type of food, but I would try anything once. The balls were filled with chicken. They tasted like sticky barbecue glaze, and inside was a whole egg that oozed perfectly as I bit into it. The combination of the three elements moved it straight to the top of the list, above the slab of omelette and the gooey melon bread.

"That was one of the nicest things I have ever tasted." I licked my lips approvingly. "I feel like I've been saying that a lot on this trip."

"You're attractive when you eat. Have I ever told you that?" Her eyes softened into a stare, and she didn't break contact.

"Are you flirting with me, Brooke Jacobs?" I became consciously aware of my facial expressions. She looked at my lips. Suddenly, licking them seemed inappropriate. I could feel my jaw tense; nothing seemed natural anymore. I felt like I was under a microscope. Nervous.

Brooke grabbed me by the hand and pulled me towards the skirted figure sign that indicated the women's toilets.

"Where are we—"

We dodged the cleaning attendant. She had impeccable timing and was just finishing up. When inside, Brooke slammed the door closed. The sharp clicking of the latch echoed as it fell into place followed immediately by *silence*.

"Does this feel familiar to you?" She grinned.

"Very." I gulped.

"Sit down." She pushed me back onto the toilet seat and straddled me either side. It was too much for my brain to handle: the adrenaline, the butterflies, the sexual tension. It all merged to create an almost out-of-body experience. It felt like a dream.

"Just like this?" I asked. My words came out a shaky exhale.

"Yes." She leant forwards and breathed softly against my neck. Her lips skimmed the side of my jaw as she whispered, "I have missed you so much."

My body froze.

My breathing was irregular.

The sensation of her skin so close to mine and her soft voice delicately purring in my ear sent a shiver down my spine, but it also caused the excruciating turn of my stomach. Suddenly my whole body felt like it was being launched from left to right in a washing machine.

She missed me.

How was I supposed to respond to that?

The obvious reply refused to leave my lips. Of course I missed her too, but before I had a chance to shake my body from its trance she was kissing me.

She was really kissing me this time, with a raw passion, and with the intensity of someone who knew it could go further. My neck, my ears, my mouth, my cheeks, she kissed me until my own lips matched her energy.

Her mouth was insistent. She knew what she wanted. Suddenly, I forgot everything, not just the inelegance of our whereabouts, or that we were reliving our first kiss, but the apprehension I felt at leaving, the bad timing of it all, and the ache. That was the big one, the constant agony I felt with every second that passed knowing my time with her was running out.

This was a dream I wished I could refuse to wake up from, but for a few minutes I forgot it all. As I felt the warm tip of her tongue trace my lips, she manoeuvred her tongue to compliment mine. Brooke was the one thing I could never forget. I needed her in order to survive.

*

We took the 12:30 p.m. train from Ginza to Nakameguro Station. The trendy neighbourhood was best known for the Meguro River that runs through it, so we walked alongside the river. It was flanked by cherry trees, independent stores selling all kinds of books and art, as well as a myriad of eateries.

We stopped at two Japanese gastropubs tucked neatly away in the narrow side streets. Each offered a different element. The need to rehydrate every thirty minutes or so made for several pit stops, although we didn't eat until we reached a little back street pizzeria that would give any Italian restaurant a run for its money. The smell hit me before I noticed the sign.

"Can you smell that?" I asked.

"It smells heavenly. I can't believe we're still hungry." Brooke laughed.

"It's hard to turn down pizza."

"Do you remember—" We both went to say the words at the same time.

"When I ordered a pizza to your office for your dinner, because you refused to go home?" She smiled.

"Yes, and you had the delivery driver write a note on the box." This was before we'd even shared our first kiss. When we claimed to be, "good friends". We'd been so much more than that.

"I did. Do you remember what it said?" Brooke asked.

We sat outside on two of the four metal chairs under the worn-out canopy.

"It said, *Maybe one day we can share a pizza together*, I think?"

"It did. And what did you do?"

"I called you into the office the next morning and offered you pizza for breakfast." I remember it so vividly. Things were so simple back then.

"You did. You even provided a piece of A4 paper from the printer as a plate and a can of Coke from the vending machine. I just knew." She pulled at her dress. There was no attempt to finish her sentence. Instead, she turned her attention to the menu.

We opted for the Margherita. The wood fired crust was perfectly charred. The little speckles of salt sprinkled over the dough and the creamy mozzarella made for a great combination. There was a hint of garlic on the base that elevated the flavour and transported me right to the small side streets of Venice.

After exploring Nakameguro for an hour or two we got a coffee to go and found a quiet spot by the river. We leant up against the railings, and I fished out the Kashi Pan with cream cheese filling from earlier.

"Surprisingly I'm not even that full. I feel like all we've done is eat," I said as I pulled the fluffy bread pastry from its box.

"That was the point of today. Wasn't it?" Brooke smirked.

"Yes. Here, you get the first bite."

"Do you really think I'm going to fall for that again?" She rolled her eyes.

"No, I wouldn't do that, honestly." I used my free hand to cross my heart. She nodded, and I proceeded to feed her.

"Mmm, that's good." She licked at her lips, and I couldn't help but smile.

"What?" She mumbled through a mouth full of bread.

"Nothing." I shrugged.

"No, tell me, Holly."

"I'm just happy."

It was true. I couldn't hold the eye contact any longer, so I focused more intently on pulling a piece of bread apart whilst I continued. "I can't think of anywhere in the world I'd rather be than here watching you politely stuff your face with pastry. Genuinely."

"Not even Bali? The Bahamas? Maldives?"

"Nope." I shook my head. The next part slipped out. "Not without you."

As soon as I said it, Brooke's face dropped. She looked concerned. I'd said too much.

"Holly . . ."

"Don't say anything. I'm sorry. It's too much. I know."

"You leave in like six days. I . . . There's something I need to say to you."

"You don't have to say anything. I know it's too difficult. I'm an idiot for thinking."

"What? What are you thinking?" Brooke stepped in closer and placed her hand in mine. "Tell me, Holly."

"There isn't anything to tell is there?" I sighed.

I placed the Kashi Pan on the wall and stared out towards the river. I felt Brooke's hand move from my neck to my cheek, turning my head to look at her.

"Do you love me?" she whispered.

"You know I do."

Hadn't I made that clear?

"Tell me," Brooke repeated. "Tell me you love me."

"I love you. I'll always love you."

That was the problem.

"Then tell me what you're thinking," she pleaded.

I got the feeling she wanted me to say something specific. Did she want another declaration of my love? For what reason? Maybe, just like I needed the mysterious clarity I'd been searching for, she needed some form of reassurance, but I couldn't understand or work out why.

Brooke softly kissed my lips. She stood with one hand tightly clasped in mine and the other playing with my necklace.

"I've never noticed this before." She manoeuvred the oblong silver pendant, twisting it in her fingers until she caught sight of the writing on the opposite side. "What's this?"

"It's just a phrase in Japanese. I saw it at a market in London about a year ago. It stood out to me." For a reason much deeper than the fashionable element of the necklace.

"Does it say—" she realised.

"*Love, always.*" I wiped my forehead. The heat was almost unbearable. We took shade under a large blossom tree, but the humidity and Brooke pressed up against me made it hard to regulate my body temperature.

"Did you get that for me?" she asks gingerly.

I should have made a joke, but instead I told the truth. "You know I did."

Brooke let go of my necklace and moved her other hand to the opposite side of my neck. She pulled my face down to meet hers. Our lips locked, and they remained that way. With each soft movement our lips intertwined effortlessly; neither of us had to adjust. It was as if our lips knew they were made for that moment.

There was no sign of the anxious panicked demeanour I'd become accustomed to in London. She didn't seem concerned word could get back to her father or her brother on my presence and our rendezvous. Strange really.

After a couple of minutes, we pulled back and I said what I wanted to say.

"I wish things could be different. I wish this didn't have to end. I don't want to spend the rest of my life wondering what if." I sighed.

"What if?" she responded.

"What if I let the love of my life walk away." I cupped her cheek with my hand. That perfect face.

"I'm scared Brooke."

"I'm scared too," she whispered.

"I'm scared that after today I may never see you again. I'm scared you'll marry someone else, have children, and live a life I will never be a part of." I turned to face the river. I didn't want her to see me cry.

"Don't do that. Don't hide from me."

"Most of all, I'm scared I will spend the rest of my life hoping and praying you'll come back to me."

The emotions overwhelmed me. I wanted to cry. I wanted to scream. I wanted to tear out my heart, so I couldn't feel anymore.

"Holly." Tears fell from Brooke's eyes. I was transported back to Nina's Cafe, to our final goodbye, to the moment I knew my life would never be the same again.

History was about to repeat itself. "I am so sorry."

"It's okay. You don't have to explain. We've done this several times before." The pain was too much to bear.

"It doesn't make it any easier," Brooke snivelled.

"I'm ready to go back now."

Brooke placed her head into my neck. The cold, wetness of her tears seeped into my skin.

Was I naive to have hope?

Would I ever stop wishing she'd change her mind?

Maybe, maybe not.

Time would tell.

CHAPTER THIRTEEN

The wooden breakfast bar in Beth's apartment almost had elbow marks from the position I'd held all morning. I was slumped on the bar with my hands propping up my chin. My appetite was none-existent. Even the temptation of the leftover melon pan had no effect. My hair was stuck to the back of my neck, making it so disgustingly greasy, Beth suggested I take a warm-up shower before my actual shower.

I'd barely slept. I didn't think it would be any different. The day before ended awkwardly. It was uncomfortable, but not in a horrible kind of way. It was more of a, "I've just been hit by a bus", realisation. Seeing Brooke was probably the worst idea I'd ever had, and it would undoubtably set me back for the next twelve months.

When I'd arrived home, I explained all to Beth. After the initial, slightly brutal commentary, she was as supportive as she ever was. She kicked Ren out and spent the evening stroking my hair whilst we watched reruns of *Grey's Anatomy*. It didn't stop the ache completely, but the doctors and nurses at Grey's had way bigger problems than I did.

Brooke sent me a text message at midnight with a single heart emoji. She sent another at 2 a.m. that said, *I love you*. I didn't reply at first, but trying to ignore her would only keep me awake longer, so I eventually sent a heart back and fell asleep for the next three hours.

The sweet smell of pancakes should've been enough to bring me back to life. The lingering vanilla smell, sweet maple syrup, and freshly baked cake, ordinarily would fill me with pure delight, especially knowing Beth had made them, but not today.

Beth placed her plate in the sink and pulled one out for me. "I knew the smell of pancakes would get you up." I regretted to inform her that I'd been up all night.

"Are you making the hangover special?" I asked.

"I certainly am." She grinned.

"With whipped cream?"

"Of course."

I licked my lips. I wanted to want them. Beth flipped the first pancake then turned her attention back to me.

"How are you feeling this morning?"

"If I'm honest, a little numb. I'll be okay though." I hoped.

Beth reached for the plate and flipped the first pancake neatly on top. She sprinkled on some small cut pieces of strawberry and banana before finishing off with a big swirl of whipped cream.

"Thank you."

"Pleasure."

She watched me intently. She wouldn't stop until I tried them. It was like primary school all over again. My mum used to glare at me until I ate the broccoli from my plate. I hated broccoli. I didn't however hate the pancakes. I picked at the edge; one mouthful wouldn't hurt.

"Are you going to see Brooke again before you leave?"

With a mouthful of food, I shrugged.

"Do you want to?"

I shrugged.

"Do you have any audible response or is that the best you've got right now?"

I shrugged again.

"Okay, I'll take that as you're enjoying my pancakes."

She rounded the breakfast bar and placed her hands on my shoulders.

"One thing is for sure. I will not have the last few days with my best friend ruined because you're feeling sorry for yourself."

My eyes widened. "Harsh."

"You need harsh. You realise the next time I see you, you'll be an auntie to this little bambino." She rubbed at her belly. "I am only a few months away from being a waddling whale that can do nothing other than eat." That mental picture made me chuckle. "Oh, I see. The thought of me waddling is what you find funny."

"I can't imagine you're ever going to waddle anywhere. You're five foot eleven with a body like a track star. I'll be surprised if anyone even notices you're pregnant."

I stuffed a large piece of pancake in my mouth, covering my lips and nose in cream.

"I hope so."

"What's the plan?" I asked.

Beth sauntered from one side of the room to the next talking about art museums, some amazing shopping complex, a high-end dining experience, and something about wealthy businessmen. I heard Roppongi several times, so I assumed that was the destination.

I would've done anything to take my mind off Brooke.

*

Choose Us

Roppongi was extremely lively, even during the d<!-- -->could only imagine what the entertainment district w<!-- -->be like at night. We went to the observation deck o a skyscraper complex. We listened intently to a well-spoken Englishman who'd clearly done his research on Tokyo and was thoroughly describing all the buildings to his partner.

We had free admission to Mori Art Museum. We spent about thirty minutes inside. I didn't understand what I should or should not find interesting, so after observing some unusual works of art we departed for a spot of shopping.

Choosing somewhere to eat for lunch consisted of Beth zooming in and out of Google Maps looking for restaurants in the vicinity. We stumbled upon a small restaurant hidden down a side street with only a discreet black sign and a vase outside the steel door.

The waiter ushered us inside. There were three options, the sushi bar, the drinks only area, or the teppanyaki counter. We opted for the teppanyaki and were taken downstairs into the basement.

The chef began preparing dishes on the hot iron plates. The air-con in the basement was perfectly chilled, allowing my body to cool. We ordered the sautéed organic vegetables to start, followed by wagyu beef fillet, and some garlic rice. The menu looked and sounded delicious. Under normal circumstances I would've been excited to devour a large portion of it, but I was only trying to appease Beth.

"Are you okay?" she asked.

"Yes." I didn't sound convincing.

"You're thinking about Brooke, aren't you?"

I nodded. If only it were a momentary thing. The truth was, she never left my mind. She hadn't since the day we met.

"Why don't you go and see her?" Beth suggested.

I thanked the chef as he placed the fried vegetable appetiser in front of me. "And say what?"

"Just tell her how you feel."

"What's the point? It's not going to change anything. I'm probably better just cutting ties now."

"Then what? Spend the rest of your life thinking about her? When you met her last week you told me you needed closure. Leaving it like this won't bring you closure," Beth said sternly.

"I know."

"I get that it's hard Holly, but you'll hate yourself if you don't leave on good terms."

My appetite had well and truly disappeared. The teppanyaki meal was about to be the biggest waste of ten-thousand yen.

"I don't know."

"Trust me. Go and meet her when she finishes work. You'll probably be surprised how happy she is to see you."

The precarious feeling that consumed my body made standing up in court during a murder trial seem like a walk in the park. The thought of seeing her made me feel sick, but the thought of not seeing her was far worse.

How had I become so addicted to heartbreak?

*

Chaos Kitchen was particularly quiet, which was to be expected on a Monday. I read a study once that said Mondays were the day people were least likely to dine out. I could understand that. After a heavy weekend of drinks and takeaway and a long day at work, the last thing I'd want to do was socialise in public. Under normal circumstances, that is. I was on holiday, so it didn't count.

I passed a flower shop near the train station. The elaborate flower displays in marble vases towered on top of crates. They were eye catching. A bouquet of cherry blossom flowers mixed with white roses got my attention. The arrangement was delicate and wrapped in light grey paper. I remembered Brooke telling me white roses were her mum's favourite flower, but on our trip to Nikko she'd told me cherry blossoms had become her favourite since moving to Japan. It was the perfect combination; some would say it was a sign.

Only four days remained until I flew back to London. I tried not to think about what that meant for us because it was painfully obvious. It was my desire to see as much of Brooke as I could before I left. She was due to finish in two hours. It was late, but my aim was to tempt her into a spontaneous dinner somewhere niche.

The Shibuya District was full of life. It was Japan's version of New York City; the city that never sleeps. Once I reached the Shibuya Parco building, I hit basement level on the lift, and I was back in one of the craziest places I'd seen on my trip.

Chaos Kitchen was hard to describe; the layout created an illusion of smoke-filled alleyways. There were small wooden stalls and red lanterns that reminded me of a place I'd been before, a food district, but I couldn't put my finger on the name. The smell of Hamburger patties filled the air, followed by a creamy sesame broth, which was likely a ramen dish. Each tiny restaurant offered a new array of smells enticing me inside, but I wasn't there to eat right away.

As I passed Campy!bar, the drag queen with the huge ginger wig moved their glasses to the end of their nose. They wolf whistled loudly and the whole bar turned to look. This action was followed by a phrase I'd never heard, but I assumed it was flattery. I waved back and smiled politely whilst walking hastily towards Sake Bar. I was embarrassed by the sudden attention.

I rubbed at my neck and checked over my shoulder every few steps. Was it normal to be so nervous? I wasn't sure. It sort of felt like a first date. I pictured my sixteen-year-old self asking a girl out at college for the first time. I remembered the trembling in my hands, the sick feeling in my stomach, the hot flushes; it all felt relative.

Last night, I'd remained wide awake tossing and turning with no sign of sleep until 2 a.m. My sleepless nights were a regular occurrence on this trip. I wanted to blame the heat, but the heat wasn't the problem. Beth, being the fantastic host she was, provided me with a fan, which meant after a few minutes I was cold enough to dive deep under the bedsheets. The heat was the excuse I told myself for my brain focusing on the only thing that seemed to defeat it: Brooke.

My way of coping with the ending of my trip was by telling myself it wasn't a big deal. It was better to have come to Tokyo and seen her than not at all, right? It gave me the *clarity* I needed.

Pfft.

Clarity. Deep down I was well aware that was bullshit. My perception wasn't clear. I still didn't understand why I wasn't enough, but on the flip side, as I strolled towards the bar, I didn't want to ruin whatever time we had left together, especially not with questions that could never be answered in my favour. I'd accepted my fate without her in it. I tried not to see this time with her as a setback. Instead, it was the inevitable ending we deserved.

I rounded the final corner to where I knew I would see her. There were two customers sat by the bar. A young man was serving fancy cocktails at lightning speed, but there was no sign of Brooke. As I approached, I held the flowers behind my back. I was mindful of the embarrassment I'd feel if she wasn't present.

"What can I get you?" asked the man behind the bar. He had kind eyes and quick reflexes. He caught a glass tumbling off the bar as he finished his question. Between serving one customer and taking instruction from the waitress, he managed to attend to me; he was good.

"Good catch." I said.

"It happens too often." He smiled.

"I'm looking for Brooke."

He nodded in acknowledgment. "And you are?"

Who was I? What was I?

"Just an old friend." I smiled.

He must've spied the flowers sticking out from behind my back because his gaze flickered to the left. I pulled them back in line, concealing them as best I could.

Why did I have to buy the big bunch?

"She just left. Takara picked her up."

"Oh." I looked at my watch. She must've finished early. "Do you know which way they went?" I asked.

"Through the exit over there on the right." He pointed at the illuminated neon exit sign with a straw. It was hard to miss. "There's a carpark out back. If you go quickly, you might catch them."

"Thank you."

"Pleasure." He grinned before knocking over some juice. He was sweet but clumsy.

I checked my phone to make sure I hadn't missed a text message. The message from that morning clearly said, *I finish at eight.*

I made my way out to the parking lot. I passed five or six people, but there was no sign of Brooke. I considered going back inside. Her friend, Takara, probably didn't know about me. A random girl turning up with flowers would require some explanation from Brooke, explanation she wouldn't want to give. I wasn't there to make her life harder than it needed to be.

I heard a woman's voice from the other side of a large concrete pillar. It sounded English. It was distorted slightly by the echo, but it had to be Brooke. As I got closer, I heard an unfamiliar woman's voice, and their conversation came into focus.

"Why? Were you hoping for someone different?" the unfamiliar woman asked.

"Don't start this again, Takara."

The response was Brooke.

I was almost behind the pillar now, still out of sight, but edging closer to their conversation. I should've revealed myself; it wasn't polite to eavesdrop.

The conversation sounded heated. They were arguing, but trying to make out the whole conversation was difficult. Only when Takara raised her voice did I get the gist. I placed my back against the column.

What do I do now? I thought.

This was a terrible idea, but I was stuck. More people made their way across the parking lot. One or two of them casually glanced my way. They probably thought I was trying to steal a car until they saw the flowers. Then each person smiled politely. I noted that down for future reference. If ever I'm defending someone who committed grand theft auto and they were carrying flowers; it was a ploy.

I bet they thought I must be surprising someone. They wouldn't be wrong. It was a surprise alright, but for me. I heard the car door open and close. I had to wait it out. Once they left the parking lot, I could take the flowers home to Beth.

I felt seedy hiding away. I was thirty years old. I shouldn't still feel like someone's secret. I rolled my head against the concrete pillar—waiting. The car engine didn't start. I heard Brooke's voice as clear as day.

"Can we just discuss this later, please?"

"Why won't you tell me what happened yesterday?" Takara sounded angry. Like really angry, which didn't sit right with me. What did she want to know about yesterday? Brooke was with me all day. Why would she be angry about that?

Unless—

No, it wasn't possible.

I desperately wanted to clear my throat, but that would alert them to my position. Was Brooke getting closer to me?

My pounding heartbeat could be felt in my temples. My body was as flat up against the pillar as it could be.

"There's nothing to tell," Brooke said.

"You're lying," Takara yelled loudly enough to project above the rumble of the nearby engines.

"Seriously, you want to do this now, in the middle of the carpark?"

Brooke sounded furious. She raised her voice to match Takara's. I'd never heard her shout. It was strange to hear her usually calm and cool voice so agitated.

This wasn't just a fall out with a friend. My gut told me different.

"Maybe you'll tell me because there's an audience."

Takara hissed. There was venom in her voice. I wanted to protect Brooke. I wanted to stand by her side and shield her from whatever this encounter was, but my brain rejected that idea.

"Do you know me at all, Takara? Do you think this is going to get me to talk to you? You're out of your mind."

I heard footsteps on the concrete.

"I'm going to get the train home."

Brooke was getting closer. There was no way out for me. Brooke lowered her voice. Spectators were gathering.

"She's not an old friend, is she?" Takara asked.

This was about me. Shit.

"Admit it, Brooke."

There was silence and then a longer than necessary pause. She was composing herself for what was to come.

"No, she isn't."

My muscles tightened. My vision blurred.

"I knew it," Takara said coldly.

I couldn't hear footsteps anymore. I glanced towards the car on my left. The reflection in the paintwork showed Brooke standing still. She didn't turn around, but I watched her pinch the bridge of her nose.

"Takara, please. Not now."

This wasn't Brooke's scene. She didn't like large public displays of the good or the bad kind.

Should I step out and say something? No. That would only make things worse.

"What then? Was she another closet relationship you refused to tell your father about? You swore to me you'd never done this before."

My chest stopped its rhythm. My breathing slowed to a halt.

"Takara!" Brooke shrieked.

Another closet relationship?

She was in a relationship with Takara? I knew something felt wrong, but hearing it out loud sent shockwaves through my entire body.

I couldn't run. I couldn't yell. I couldn't do anything other than stand and listen to my worst nightmare.

"Will you keep your voice down," Brooke hissed.

Naively, I'd assumed Brooke would go back to men, not that it would make the revelation any nicer on my ears, but I assumed she'd marry traditionally and have kids. The possibility of her being with another woman never crossed my mind.

The betrayal.

I held my elbows tight to my sides and only made small movements. I needed to wake my body from the paralyzing ache.

She wasn't mine anymore, but I'd assumed a part of her always would be.

The revelation changed everything.

CHAPTER FOURTEEN

"Are you okay? You look lost?" a sweet Japanese lady hollered from the wound down window of her Honda Civic. It wasn't the time for small talk. I nodded, hoping she would understand I did not wish to be interacted with.

She did not. "Are you sure?"

I waved my hand rudely. "Yes, thanks."

"What did you say?" She leaned further, so her head was practically sticking out of the car.

"You have got to be kidding me," I muttered under my breath.

What was wrong with this woman? I tried to shoo her away. Couldn't she see I was hiding? Clearly, I wanted no part of the conversation. The caring nature of a local was not what I wanted to experience at that moment. It felt harsh, and I would probably pay for it in hell, but trying not to get caught by Brooke was my priority.

"I'm okay, thank you," I whispered.

Her confused facial expression told me she still didn't understand what I was saying or if I was telling the truth. She shook her head before driving off at speed. She may well have gone and rung the police alluding to someone acting suspicious or potentially in danger. That was the least of my worries.

Actually, the police arriving at that moment would've been ideal. Being whisked away in the back of a police car sounded appealing. I'd have done anything to get out of the carpark of doom.

I spun to my left. I couldn't see Brooke in the reflection anymore. I stealthily made my way around the pillar. I was now blind to whatever drama was unfolding between Brooke and Takara

Please don't be there. Please don't be there.

The four concrete walls seemed to be closing in around me with every second that passed. I didn't have time to think. The tightening in my chest confirmed what I'd heard, but I would deal with that later. My only concern was getting out unseen. I didn't need to make a bigger fool of myself.

Just make a decision, I screamed in my head.

I needed her to either get in the car and leave or walk out of the carpark. After the third person in five minutes looked in my direction, I knew it was time to make a run for it. I was a sitting duck, waiting to be humiliated.

I couldn't hear Brooke anymore. Or Takara.

I had to make my move.

One—you can do this.

Two—you can do this.

Three—go.

I set off walking rapidly towards the carpark exit. I kept my head down and my posture hunched. My hands were sweating. My forehead felt damp. The imprint of the flowers' stems carved into my hand as I gripped them tighter. They'd drooped slightly; they too felt sorry for me.

There was a bin in the corner by the door. I made a beeline for it.

"Holly?"

Gulp.

I ignored my name being called and told myself, just keep walking.

"Holly." This time it was a lot louder and more desperate.

Ignore it.

I was a stone's throw from the exit. On the other side of the steel door was my safe haven and my escape from the carpark of my nightmares.

Just keep walking.

A man tapped my arm as I passed by. "Excuse me, I think that lady is calling you."

"Yep, got that," I whispered. "Thank you."

He walked off pleased with himself. He probably thought he was doing a nice thing. Little did he know he'd just single-handedly blown what was left of my cover and forced me to face probably the most awkward conversation of my entire existence.

I could've kept walking.

I didn't owe Brooke. If anything, she owed me an explanation, and if I chose to walk away and not hear it that was up to me.

My legs edged forward. Step by step. They wanted to keep going, but the resistance was too strong. I couldn't turn around.

What if I just pretended it wasn't me?

I'm sure there's plenty of women in Japan with brown hair and a similar body shape. I could pretend, run away, escape to Beth's apartment and text Brooke on my flight back to London in a few days' time saying, *Thank you for the memories, but I think we should cut ties, and no I wasn't stalking you in a carpark with a bunch of flowers. That would be absurd.*

When I heard her voice call out again, she was much closer.

"Holly, I know it's you." She sighed.

There was no getting out of it now.

I spun around in one fluid motion, adjusting the flowers in the process and holding them tight to my back and hidden.

"What are you doing here?" Brooke asked.

I looked over her shoulder. I could see Takara leant against the boot of her car, arms folded. All she needed was a toothpick and a packet of cigarettes rolled in her sleeve to finish off the badass look.

She wasn't what I'd expected, but now that I knew she was gay it made sense. The short boyish cut swept across her face like a Justin Bieber hairstyle from 2010. She was skinny and probably the same height as me. She wore a grey shirt with the sleeves rolled up and some skinny black jeans. I wasn't close enough to admire her features, but she looked like she had great bone structure.

"I came to get some food." I bowed my head, kicking at the small pebbles on the concrete floor.

"Did Beth drive you here?"

"No, I got the train. I just got lost looking for the toilets." I shrugged.

"Huh, so you came here alone?" Brooke brushed a strand of hair behind her ear. She wouldn't hold my gaze.

"Yes, I like to eat alone." It wasn't a complete lie.

"Seriously, Holly? Are we really doing this?" She clasped her own arm with her hand.

"Okay, so I came to see you." I sighed.

"Oh." She turned back to look at Takara who was watching the entire exchange with a sour face. "I thought after yesterday you wouldn't want to see me again."

"Yeah, well I'm an idiot, so," I snapped back. She ignored my remark.

"What are you hiding behind your back?" Brooke asked gently.

"Nothing," I mumbled.

"You are. Let me see." She smiled playfully. Did she think the whole thing was a game?

I pulled the perfectly nice flowers from behind my back, walked the remaining two paces to the bin, and dumped them dramatically.

"You bought me flowers?"

"They're irrelevant now."

"You didn't have to throw them away, Holly. Were they—"

"Your favourite? Yes, they were because I listen, and I am thoughtful, and I thought maybe you hadn't been lying to me this entire time."

Brooke didn't say a word. I gestured angrily towards Takara.

"Are we not going to discuss the fact that you've got a girlfriend who happens to be standing right over there?" I eyeballed Takara. She adjusted her position.

Brooke's eyes widened. "What did you hear?"

"Enough."

"You have to let me explain."

"Go on then."

"Now's not a good time, but we have to talk about this, Holly. You owe me that, at least."

"I owe you?" I sneered. "That's rich."

"Please. I just want to make things right."

"Save it, Brooke. Nothing about this will ever be right."

"Please, Holly. You see everything so black and white, but it's not that simple."

She looked back towards Takara who was unmoving.

"You better get back to your girlfriend before she gets upset."

I turned to leave, but she grabbed me by the hand.

"Holly. Please . . . don't do this," she begged.

Her eyes glistened. For a second, I almost felt sorry for her.

"Goodbye, Brooke."

I yanked my hand free and walked as fast as I could out of the parking lot and away from the shopping complex. I held my head high, trying to maintain some shred of self-respect.

Had she played me?

Was any of it real?

The thing I struggled with most when we broke up was the thought of being an experiment, just another notch on the bedpost, as they say.

Maybe I was her gateway into the world of being a lesbian, and now she was honing her skills halfway around the world with the next woman to be sucked into her closeted world of lies.

*

It took over an hour to get back to Beth's apartment. I thought about calling her, but the journey alone on the train gave me time to reflect. There were tears, and I had no doubt there would be more. The tissue I'd picked up from the coffee cart was now sodden and torn to pieces in my pocket. My reflection in the downstairs window of the apartment building I passed highlighted my red puffy eyes. Beth would know instantly that I was upset, and I wasn't sure I had the strength to discuss it, never mind to pretend any different.

The apartment was eerily quiet when I wandered inside. Normally, the TV would be blaring, or there'd be music playing. Beth would usually greet me by bellowing my name at the top of her lungs, but this time there was nothing. When I rounded the corner to the living area, I saw Beth first. She sat on the edge of the sofa, visibly uncomfortable. She looked at me with concern in her eyes and a smile that screamed pity.

Beth's eyes flashed to her right. Someone else was there. The smell hit me first. I would recognise her scent anywhere. Before I clocked the long blonde hair I knew she was there.

The second person came into view.

Brooke.

"What is she doing here?" I aimed my question at Beth.

"I'm sorry. It seemed urgent," Beth apologised. It was my fault for not texting her. If I'd given her some warning she might not have let her in. Then again, how was I to know Brooke would teleport into Beth's living room.

"I want to talk to you, Holly. Please." Brooke had her arms crossed tightly against her chest.

"What exactly is there to talk about?" I scowled. I placed my hands in my pockets to disguise the shaking. "It all makes perfect sense to me now."

"It's not that simple." Brooke pursed her lips; her brow was defined. The pain looked genuine, but was it just guilt?

"I don't need your explanation." I sniffled.

Beth stood. "I think you two need some time alone, so I'm going to take a drive. I'll see you later." Beth grabbed her car keys from the kitchen counter and gently placed her hand on my arm as she passed. "Call me if you need me," she whispered.

The door slammed shut.

We were alone.

Brooke walked to the edge of the sofa and propped herself up against the arm. She was poised and ready. All

I wanted was to get a shower, wallow in self-pity, and cry myself to sleep. I couldn't do any of that with Brooke standing there.

I slumped on the bar stool and folded my arms abruptly but remained silent. I wanted with all my heart to be angry, to cuss at her, throw some fruit from the fruit bowl, or storm out dramatically calling her a liar, but none of that was realistic.

All I felt was pain.

She didn't speak. I didn't speak. The air between us was heavy with questions, reason, and uncertainty, but neither of us seemed to know how to make the first move.

"So, you have a girlfriend?" Saying the words out loud made me feel nauseous. "I've got to say, I didn't expect that while I was fucking you in the back of your car." I hissed. "Real nice, Brooke."

She bowed her head. "I deserved that." She sighed.

I pinched at my arm.

Regain some composure.

It was pitch black outside. The light from the TV and a small undermount light in the kitchen were the only two things illuminating the apartment. I didn't make any attempt to change the poor lighting. If anything, it was doing me a favour hiding my eyes.

"How long have you been together?" I asked.

Brooke sighed. "Six months."

"Wow. It's serious." The weight of the situation was crushing my soul. "So, are you a lesbian now?" I asked through gritted teeth.

"I don't think it's that simple." The more she evaded, the angrier I felt.

"I mean, it's pretty simple, Brooke." I picked up my phone. The screen had a couple of work emails and a three hour late reply from my mum about what happened on the latest episode of *Hollyoaks*, but nothing else. I wanted a distraction, anything to take me away from the nightmare unfolding before me.

"Holly."

"Here I was thinking I was the only girl you would ever love. That's what you told me wasn't it? Here's me thinking I was special, and what we had would always be between me and you. Then you move to Japan and shack up with the first girl you come across."

I couldn't stay seated. My leg bounced up and down against the footrest. I raced to the fridge. My throat was dry and rough.

"It's not like that." She gave the same generic answer; it seemed to be her new go to.

"You're talking a lot, Brooke, but you're not saying anything."

"I know. I just don't know what to say for the best. I want to be honest. I don't want to make things worse, but it's easier said than done."

I poured myself a glass of wine, anything to take the edge off. The lump in my throat felt like I was trying to swallow a golf ball. The next question was on the tip of my tongue.

"Are you not in a sexual relationship with Takara?" I had my back to Brooke. My eyes clenched tightly. I didn't want to know the answer, not really, but it seemed I was in the mood to cause myself pain.

"Yes, I am, but . . ." Her voice faded.

My cheeks blushed as the heat blazed through my entire body.

"But what?" I snapped.

"I'm not in love with her, Holly," she said, tenderly.

Don't believe her. No good can come from this.

The pain I felt at not being chosen by her two years ago had been more than I could abide. At the time I felt I might never love again. I might never be the same ever again. The thought of her choosing someone else, introducing her to her dad, or that person being the one she gave up everything for; it was so much worse.

"Just leave, Brooke. I don't want to hear anymore." I pinched the bridge of my nose.

Don't get upset. Stay strong.

"Can I at least explain before I go?" Brooke asked.

I still couldn't look at her. The wine hit the back of my throat with a bitter taste. She didn't give me a chance to respond.

"I wanted to tell you about Takara on more than one occasion, but you can't blame me for not being able to find the right words." She paused. "She was the first friend I made in Japan. If I'm honest, I didn't see her as anything other than that. She told me she was gay about a year ago. I thought about telling her about you, at least she'd understand, but after a while I started to feel her energy change towards me. I thought she might like me, and I didn't want to give her any reason to think I might be interested." Brooke strolled to the window and began fiddling with the blinds. I said nothing.

"About six months ago I got very drunk, and I let her kiss me. The next day I knew it was a bad idea, but I couldn't take it back, so I tried to play it off for a few weeks. I guess, over time I became curious. I had the opportunity to see what it would be like with another woman, to see if she could make me feel anything like how *you* made me feel."

"And did she?" I gulped. I didn't think I had ever felt my brain swell in my head until that moment. I feared it might be tight enough to cause severe damage.

"No." Brooke sighed. "Not even close."

"What about now?" I didn't want to know, but my stupid mouth kept asking questions. Maybe it was self-sabotage. The more I felt hurt, the less likely I was to go back. Thinking about her kissing Takara every time she moved her lips didn't stop me wanting to explore her entire body with my hands.

Stop it, I screamed internally.

Brooke remained tight lipped.

"Do you love her?" I asked.

She didn't answer right away.

"I care . . . for her."

It was a cop out if I'd ever heard one.

"Don't you feel guilty?"

"For which part?" Brooke looked me dead in the eye.

"You've spent the last week skipping down memory lane with me, doing what we've done, and you don't feel guilty? If I'd known you were with someone else—" I broke away mid-sentence. I was getting on my high horse, and I was acutely aware of it. I walked to the fridge and rummaged for more wine.

"What, Holly? You wouldn't have spent time with me? You wouldn't have kissed me or told me you still loved me?" She was visibly annoyed now, which I thought was laughable. How could she be annoyed at me?

"Maybe not," I said hesitantly. It was the most unconvincing response I'd ever given. If I was in a court of law, I would've been ripped to pieces.

"I find that hard to believe." Brooke huffed.

"Talk about being full of yourself." I sneered.

Her eyes narrowed. "You're impossible sometimes. Do you know that?"

"I'm impossible? What have I done?" Brooke literally had a woman in every country as part of her closeted life of lies, and I was impossible? I laughed.

"Yes, because you can't for one second get your head out of your ass to see how difficult this is for me."

"Please enlighten me as to how this is difficult for you?"

My second glass of wine went down the hatch in one gulp. It seemed there was no better time to get blind drunk and forget all about the events of the past ten days.

"You can sit there and tell me you would've done things differently, or you would've been more honest, but it doesn't matter because what's done is done. I tried to ignore you. I tried to carry on walking that day in Shibuya. I tried to stop myself from seeing you again. I tried to resist kissing you, having sex with you, holding you, and touching you, but I couldn't, okay? Is that what you want to hear? I am so weak when it comes to you I found it physically impossible not to want you." Her voice broke.

I slammed the glass down on the counter harder than I'd intended. She flinched. This was what I'd feared in coming to Japan, seeing her again, and letting myself feel as deeply as I once had for her.

There was one more question I had to ask. My body fought against me. The vein in my forehead pulsated at the sheer vulnerability of the situation. The moment she left I knew I would burst into tears.

"Why wasn't I enough for you?"

There it was—the golden question. The answer would be the start of my recovery and my journey to a Brooke free life.

She flinched. My words struck a nerve. "You were enough for me."

"That's a lie, Brooke."

She stepped forward, edging closer. "My decision to stand by my dad wasn't a reflection on you, Holly."

I laughed sarcastically. "How can you say that? What was it then?"

"The hardest decision I ever had to make." She sighed.

Brooke walked towards me; only the kitchen counter filled with fruit, glasses, and a small green plant that gave off a strong citrus scent, separated us.

"Bullshit." My voice sounded unfamiliar to me. It was hoarse, broken, and growing harsher the louder it became. I didn't recognise myself.

She grimaced. "Holly."

"No. I can't do this anymore. Everything you've ever said to me was a lie. If you loved me, you would've risked everything to be with me, even if that meant not babysitting your homophobic condescending asshole of a father." I slammed the bottle back in the fridge and threw my arm out towards the door.

"Just leave, Brooke."

"But—

"Leave," I yelled.

I watched the tears form in her eyes. My body began trembling. I was overcome with emotion. I willed my hands to stop shaking. The room felt like it was closing in around me. It might have been two years, but my face burned bright with the thought of Brooke's betrayal. It should've been easier.

I wanted her to walk out the door, but my legs buckled, and I could've dropped to my knees. I wanted to beg her to stay. My head and my heart were submerged in a giant body of water that acted as a metaphor for the emotional turmoil I couldn't shake or process. There was no way to tread water anymore.

This was it.

The end.

She took two long strides towards the door. She stopped in place; her hand hovered over the door handle. She looked back at me. I averted my gaze.

Don't let her break you, again.

"For what it's worth, not a day has gone by that I haven't thought about you. You consume my mind more than I thought humanly possible. I thought moving to Japan would help me move on, but all I've done is move my life and my body. My heart is still with you in London."

She smiled. It felt genuine. That small gesture was all it took for the iron clad walls around my heart to fall once again.

She continued.

"I don't think I will ever be the same, knowing I found you, and I let you go. You may never understand, but I had to make a choice. I will resent my father for the rest of my life for being the one to instigate that choice, but here I am, and I can't take it back." She sighed.

I had to fight the urge to embrace her.

"Spending time with you again has been magical. It's a time I will never forget. Apart from maybe this argument." She smiled softly. Tears rolled down her face.

Brooke opened the door and stepped out over the threshold. She turned back one last time; her T-shirt was covered in tear stains. Her mouth quivered. Her eyes looked dull and absent.

"I love you, Holly."

The latch on the door clicked into place, and she was gone.

"*I love you too*," I whispered.

I watched through the blinds in the kitchen as she took a right towards the train station. The vision of her walking away would haunt my dreams for years. I slumped to the floor and let out an almighty cry.

CHAPTER FIFTEEN

I've heard people say, "timing is everything", especially when it comes to relationships. I genuinely believed I'd met the right person in Brooke, and I'd just met her at the wrong time. It sucked for me, but that was reality, right? She seemed perfect, but the extenuating circumstances pulled us apart. That's the way the cookie crumbled, or in my case, shattered.

My experience in Japan changed my view. Was bad timing just an excuse for the demise of a relationship? Surely, if she was the right person for me the timing wouldn't matter? Surely, any obstacles or homophobic parents standing in the way of our happiness should be irrelevant, right?

The hardest part was knowing we could've been so much more. We never had the chance to explore the depths of our connection fully. We'd barely started. My experience left me in limbo, as I prepared to return home.

I believed time would slowly heal my wounds, a plaster here, a bandage there, but without invasive surgery would my hypothetical wound ever fully heal? What would be the surgery? Was it time to accept that not everything works out like the movies, regardless of how seemingly matchless someone might be for me?

Life was too short; the older I got the more that saying rang true. I had spent the last two years of my life pining over Brooke, desperately hoping by some miracle that she would find her way back to me. Now there was nothing left to cling to. There was nothing else to do. I had to move on.

The hopeless romantic in me held on to a small belief that if we were meant to be we would find a way. It was what Beth told me the previous night as I sobbed in her arms. I was positive that's what Paula would tell me too. My mum would recite some version of the same old story about meeting my dad when she was seventeen on a family holiday in Majorca. They'd lost touch for ten years only to meet again in the same area of Majorca. Did my dad stalk her? Potentially, and I teased him about it often.

The universe had a way of bringing two people who were meant to be in each other's lives together. Holding on to that hope made the pain somewhat bearable, but it wouldn't help me now. It was hard to forget I'd been replaced. That changed everything.

After waving a sad goodbye to my best friend at the entrance to the departure terminal, I knew the next time I saw Beth in person, she'd have another little person to care for. I would be cool Aunt Holly, and there would be one more reminder I wasn't getting any younger. The only constant in my life was the caramel macchiato I had every morning on my way to work.

The return flight always seemed longer. I think it was my body's way of preparing itself for my return to work. The pilots must know, maybe they take a slight detour because they feel sorry for the mind-numbing normality everybody is about to return to when they step foot off the plane. I tried not to dwell, but reading my emails only made that harder. Work would be a good distraction, I told myself.

Four hours into the flight and I was on my fourth gin and tonic. The more intoxicated I was, the sleepier I became, and the world around me felt more tolerable. A man behind me thought it was necessary to play a game on his laptop with the sound turned up to a socially unacceptable volume. The flight attendant kindly asked him to turn it down, but he was entitled and insisted he had a deadline to meet and didn't want to wear headphones because they hurt his ears.

The man to the left of me was snoring louder than a herd of sleeping hippos, not that I'd heard hippos snore, but I would take a guess and say they're probably loud. I'd become the considerate passenger who wore their headphones, mainly because I didn't want to subject the whole of business class to the sing-along version of *Aladdin*; it was my idea of a great film.

The constant supply of food helped curb my irritation. It was strange having a smoked salmon and asparagus starter followed by braised lamb shank all before eleven thirty in the morning, but the food was beautiful for plane food. It was a solid ten out of ten. The time difference was about to ruin my routine for at least the next two days, so as soon as my eyelids felt heavy, I forced myself to sleep.

*

When someone asked me what my favourite something was, I responded with ease. It was a simple question. A few weeks ago, someone at work asked what had been my favourite case to work on. I responded without hesitation; it was 100 percent the Russell v Crane case of 2017.

On the flight home the attendant noticed my delight at the vast movie selection on the in-flight entertainment system.

"What's your favourite film?" She smiled politely.

I pointed towards the blue *Avatar* in the top left corner of the list.

"*Avatar*? Interesting."

"What about you?" I asked, making conversation. She clearly didn't have a lot to do in our cabin; the majority of the passengers were sleeping.

"It's not on here, but my favourite has always been *E.T.*"

It was a solid choice.

She was friendly, but the favourite film question was one of many triggers. Brooke's favourites were also my favourites.

Her favourite colour—*Purple*.

Her favourite film—*Avatar*.

Her favourite cuisine—*Chinese*.

Her favourite dessert—*Apple Pie*.

Her favourite drink—*Hot Chocolate*. But only with marshmallows and whipped cream.

I was curious to know if she had new favourites. Had Japan changed her identity? Was her new favourite dessert mochi? Was her favourite food now the *tamagoyaki*? Did she have all these new experiences and likes I could no longer relate to?

It was a hard pill to swallow.

Our compatibility had never been in question before, but there was a distance between us now; it felt like a million miles. It wasn't just the physical distance from London to Japan, but a mental distance tugging me away from the picturesque dream-like world where I'd kept her locked away. I'd held on to the fantasy of her return.

The second I touched down on British soil a phone call from Paula caused excessive vibrations on the tray table. When I said the second, I wasn't exaggerating. I didn't answer the first time whilst I was in the midst of scrambling my way off the plane.

"I swear that woman has a tracking device on me," I muttered.

After twenty minutes I had three texts to accompany the phone calls. Did she not understand baggage claim?

Paula
Call

Paula
Me

Paula
Now

Anyone who didn't know Paula would assume she was in serious trouble, or she'd just bumped into *the* Adele in the middle of Harrods. I would bet my life the real situation was far less exciting.

"Hi, Paula."

"Holly! What took you so long? Your flight got in thirty minutes ago," she screeched.

"Are you stalking me?" I laughed.

"Duh, there's a flight tracker online. I've been excited for your return."

"Can we not talk about work though? Just for a day. I'd like nothing more than to sleep, eat and—"

"Come out for a drink with me?" she interrupted excitedly.

"I was going to say shower."

I dodged a woman with a double buggy and a suitcase taking up the width of four people. The weather in London had been exceeding twenty-five degrees for the past two weeks. Today was no different. It was a nice welcome home.

"Please? Just one?"

"I'm tired." I yawned. "And it's never just one. When was the last time we went out for *one* drink?"

"We do it all the time." Paula scoffed.

"A coffee break at work doesn't count."

"It's still a drink," she said, all smug. "Listen, I know you will have taken full advantage of the bed in first class, so don't give me the whole I'm tired speech."

I had actually, for about four hours. It was bliss, but I'd travelled through the night and four hours sleep was not enough.

"A little, but my mind has been too preoccupied to sleep." I realised what I'd said as soon as I'd said it. I'd given her a way in. I loved Paula, but I wanted to get home, kick off my shoes, launch my suitcase in the spare room to deal with another day, and curl up in front of the TV with a long stemmed, large glass of wine and a boxset, ideally something scary or funny, not romantic—God no. That would be bad.

"Exactly, so there's no point lying awake trying to sleep when you can come and see me."

"Fine. No work talk please. And no Brooke talk, or Francesca talk." I didn't have the energy for any of the above.

She tutted. "Well, what am I supposed to ask you about then?"

"The weather, the news, Netflix, Jeremey's latest mishaps. Anything that doesn't give me anxiety or make me want to cry."

Basically, the boring stuff.

"Right, well I'll not talk about *This Is Us* then." I assumed she was referring to the TV show. How many episodes are in that show? I wondered. She's been binge watching it for months.

"Are you still crying at the acting? Or the fact you'll never be married to Justin Hartley?"

"Both. I watched three episodes last night and no word of a lie, it was like something out of a nineties romcom. I sat with a box of tissues, some ice cream, and wiped the tears away with the old sweater I was wearing from my university days. You should have seen me; it was a picture. Oh god, this one scene was unbelievable. I'll not tell you because I don't want to ruin it if you ever watch it, but my god, my heart broke." She fake cried on the other end of the line. I could comfortably say I wouldn't be watching it anytime soon. I needed to stop crying, not cry more.

"Why watch it then? If it breaks your heart and makes you cry like a baby." I laughed.

"Because it's INCREDIBLE," she yelled the last part so loudly I had to pull the phone away from my ear.

"I'll take your word for it. Where am I meeting you?"

I felt bad for sounding unenthusiastic. Any other day I would've been happy to meet Paula and "chew the fat" as she so often said—I really hated that expression.

Today was different.

Today was glum.

"The Botanist?" she suggested.

"The bar by Sloan Square?"

"Yes, that's the one. We went once with the work gang. It's mine and Jeremy's new favourite spot."

"That's where I had the strawberry mojito isn't it?"

"Yes, the one you spoke about for three months after."

"Okay, I'm sold."

Paula chuckled. "Perfect, see you there."

*

The Botanist was one of the more elegant bars I'd been to. It was a two-minute walk from the tube station, ideal really. The modern interior was perfect for a chic cocktail bar, but it was also the type of place that could host a canapé reception, a quiet lunch, or a suave business meeting. It catered for all occasions.

Paula was waiting outside when I arrived, as prompt as ever. I noticed her from across the street because you don't get many short, red-haired women with killer heels and the eccentric dress sense of a Gucci ambassador at the MET gala. I was only envious she could pull off green and red like the two colours weren't supposed to be mortal enemies. Everybody knows red and green should never be seen.

What I didn't notice until I got closer was the two figures stood to her left. She wasn't shy of talking to a stranger or two, but she laughed and joked with them as though they belonged. When she saw me approaching and waved frantically, they turned, and their identities were revealed.

It was Francesca and Ashleigh.

I would notice those high cheekbones anywhere. I was going to kill Paula, but first I told myself to smile and wave back.

"Sorry I'm a few minutes late," I said through gritted teeth.

"I don't know why you still apologise." Paula laughed. She embraced me with wide open arms giving me the perfect opportunity to whisper in her ear. "You've ambushed me."

"You can kill me later," Paula responded.

"I will."

I pulled away smiling politely at the company I had been blissfully unaware would be joining us.

"Ashleigh." I nodded. She pulled me in for a hug.

"We've missed you at work."

"I doubt that."

She was being polite.

"Are you kidding? There's only one lawyer that gets shit done, and that's you. Do you know we've had cheap coffee beans in the machine for the past seven days because we ran out and nobody dared ask Mr. West for £100 to get that beautiful roasted blend you get from the market."

"Seriously, Holly. If you don't fix that and I have to hear Ashleigh mention it one more time I'm going to throw the coffee machine out of the window." Paula rolled her eyes.

"My coffee fix is important, Paula!" Ashleigh said.

"I'll sort it for you next week. Don't panic." I laughed. Yes, £100 was excessive for coffee beans, but the taste was worth it.

I turned my attention to Francesca. "Hey, Francesca."

"Hi, Holly." The soothing sound of her Italian accent made me perk up instantly. I hugged her too; it was only polite to do so.

"How long's it been? About six months?"

"Your thirtieth birthday," Francesca clarified. The wind blew her hair from left to right, which only enhanced her appearance; even the wind worked in her favour. How did she do that?

"Oh, of course." I smiled.

Awkward silence.

Paula changed the subject. "Shall we go inside?"

I nodded eagerly. The bar was fairly quiet, the service quick, and within five minutes I had a strawberry mojito in my hand. I got the feeling that Francesca hadn't known I was coming. Paula was up to her sneaky ways again. When Ashleigh excused herself to go to the toilet, Francesca accompanied her, as all good friends do, and I took my opportunity to accost Paula.

"What are you doing?" I scowled.

"I don't know what you mean." She hid behind her drink.

"Paula, whatever game you're playing, stop it."

"Oh, come on. I can see the chemistry between you two. I figured you could use some fun, someone to make you feel good about yourself, and who knows maybe it'll turn into something more." She shrugged.

"Paula, I appreciate you trying to cheer me up, but I am nowhere near ready for that. I am so far away from that I'm not even in the same galaxy." I glanced towards the toilet, no sign of them yet.

"Oh." She sulked. "I'm fed up of seeing you upset all the time."

"You act like I walk around snotting and crying."

"You might as well, your face is a giant sign that reads, *Don't talk to me, I'm heartbroken.* I don't like it."

"Oh great, I didn't realise I'd turned into a bleak joyless billboard." I drank the remainder of my second mojito. The cold strawberry liqueur mixed with the mint taste slowly soothed my throat. "What makes you think Francesca would even be interested. She knows I'm still in love with you know who."

"I have no idea. It's not like you have any good qualities."

"Gee, thanks." I threw a small piece of ice. It ricocheted off her drink and bounced back in my lap—karma.

"Francesca did tell Ashleigh something though—" Paula trailed off.

"What?"

"She still thinks about you, and she wishes one day you'll be over you know who, so you two could give it another try."

"She said that?" My eyes widened.

"Nope, but you liked the idea didn't you?" Paula smirked.

"You're an asshole."

Paula chuckled. "Sorry, I couldn't resist."

"Listen, Paula." I placed my hand on her arm, addressing her honestly. "I appreciate this, but I'm not ready yet. I wish I could forget her, but I can't, and I don't know how long it will take."

When it was time to put the jokes to one side, Paula could always offer a wholesome and understanding conversation.

"You take your time, Hol. I just wanted you to see how appealing you are that's all. You have a hot Italian woman that would be with you given half the chance. Your heart will heal at its own pace, but don't ever think it's her or nothing, okay?"

"Thanks, Paula."

"Anytime."

Our glasses went together with a clink. I was lucky to have Beth and Paula in my life.

I watched Francesca stroll over from the ladies' room.

Her long hair bounced. Her slender body moved with such conviction. She was a good woman, an extremely attractive woman, and if she was still interested, and that was a big if, it wouldn't be fair to lead her down a dead-end path.

I had to do the right thing for me. I needed time to heal, to learn to be happy with myself, and to be at peace with mine and Brooke's fate before I could think about being with someone else. All that was easier said than done, with no forecasted timescale. My emotional life was looking to be a perplexing puzzle I couldn't solve.

CHAPTER SIXTEEN

The Wilde v Carlton case seemed like a sure-fire win. I had evidence corroborating my client Mr. Wilde's story. He was the victim not the perpetrator, but the case took an unexpected turn when the assailant who attacked Mr. Wilde claimed his actions were not only self-defence, but retaliation because he was sexually assaulted by Mr. Wilde at the urinal prior to the incident.

My job was to weigh the factors and develop a strategy that was most likely to succeed. I was confident with my clients credibility after a lengthy conversation detailing his version of events; I thoroughly believed his explanation of what happened. He was a kind and believable man with no criminal record. I was fairly confident the jury would believe him too.

The witness testimonies were harder to come by; there was nobody with Mr. Wilde at the scene. There was nobody at the urinal at the same time, so there was nobody to corroborate his story. The only witness testimonies we had were character testimonies. They aimed to prove that the idea of Mr. Wilde committing sexual assault was ludicrous.

The provable facts were simple.

Mr. Wilde was assaulted—the physical injuries and the CCTV evidence proved this.

Mr. Wilde was alone at the urinal with the assailant—CCTV evidence inside the pub saw Mr. Wilde enter first followed quickly by the assailant.

What couldn't be proved was the alleged sexual assault. They were only alone in the toilet for three minutes before another gentleman walked in. When that gentleman was questioned, he recalled nothing out of the ordinary other than Mr. Wilde leaving in a hurry.

The police reports didn't throw out any errors that I could see. The defences strategy was simple—self-defence. People were allowed to use "reasonable force" to defend themselves, but they were not allowed to carry on attacking someone when they were no longer in danger. Mr. Carlton attacked Mr. Wilde unprovoked; the CCTV showed that.

The opening statement was critical to any case. Jurors often make up their minds about a case right after the opening statement, so it was vital I started strong and contradicted as much of the defence's opening statement as possible. I spent a lot of time preparing my opening statements, but sometimes it was the bits you didn't prepare that turned out to be the most effective.

Judge Baron sat stiffly in the judge's bench. She had on a pair of petite rectangular glasses which sat on the end of her pointed nose. Her permed grey hair looked freshly cut, not a curl was out of place. Her facial expression rarely changed. With some judges you could see the humanity in their faces, the emotion that consumed us all, but with Judge Baron, her lips remained tight, her eyes wide and observant, nothing ever slipped past her. She knew every trick in the book.

She gestured to me, "Miss Garland, please provide the court with your opening statement."

I nodded. "Thank you, your honour."

I slipped from behind the mahogany desk, taking one last glance at my notes strewn across it. I buttoned up the jacket of my pinstripe grey suit, a solid choice that morning because the defence attorney wore a navy-blue suit, which would've been my first choice had I not forgotten to pick it up from the dry cleaners. My hair was poker straight and recently cut. I made an effort for court.

"Good afternoon, my name is Holly Garland. On May 21st, 2021, the victim in this matter, Mr. Wilde, was severely assaulted. That is a fact. The evidence you see today will prove that. The defence will argue the reason he was assaulted was in retaliation. I will prove today through several witness testimonies and evidence that this isn't true." I pointed towards Mr. Wilde for dramatic effect.

"Members of the jury, this case is simple. Mr. Wilde is the victim here, not the perpetrator. Mr Carlton's accusation of sexual assault came from nowhere, an accusation several witnesses will testify is completely out of character for Mr. Wilde and frankly not believable. The defence informed you in their opening statement that they have witness testimonies, one in particular who claims to have found Mr. Carlton visibly distressed in the urinal moments before he goes out and beats Mr. Wilde in the parking lot, but what the defence failed to tell you was their witness has a history of lying to the police, and a criminal record which we will address further."

I walked before the Jury acknowledging them one by one; eye contact was key.

"The defence will try to convince you the alleged sexual assault in the urinal was Mr. Carlton's motive. Why else would he conduct himself in such a way?"

I pause for effect.

"Three fractures, yes three. Imagine how much force someone must use to cause that kind of damage. You can see the scarring on the side of Mr. Wilde's face as he sits here today. That scarring will haunt him for the rest of his life."

The jurors' eyes flicked to Mr. Wilde.

"What was the motive? It's simple. According to his defence, Mr. Carlton is a happily married man, but he is also known to frequent dating apps. I'm not here to judge Mr. Carlton on his extracurricular activities outside of his marriage, but the evidence will prove Mr. Carlton was known to partake in homosexual behaviour."

There was a faint gasp from the courtroom; I didn't turn to see the origin, but I imagine it involved someone on Mr. Carlton's side.

"I have several witness testimonies that will paint a picture for you. It is a picture of a man trapped in a marriage, a man unable to accept his true sexual identity, a man who attempted to make advances on Mr. Wilde, and a man who was met with rejection. That would bruise any man's ego, right? Even worse it would cause Mr. Carlton to panic. The fear of Mr. Wilde walking into the pub and telling people he'd had advances made by the "cock" of the town would ruin Mr. Carlton's reputation. Instead, Mr. Carlton followed Mr. Wilde into the parking lot and beat him half to death."

I let those words sink in. Mr. Carlton refused to make eye contact with me, but I knew I'd hit a nerve.

"Members of the jury, please consider all the evidence put before you. At the conclusion of this trial I will ask you to find my client not guilty."

The rest of the day went smoothly. Fully in my favour? I wasn't sure, but I was quietly confident. Mr. Carlton's defence based a large part of their argument around the police statement Mr. Wilde had provided. The original statement claimed there was no sexual assault or any advances by either party. After speaking with my office, Mr. Wilde agreed to alter his statement to contain the full truth. I had to convince the jury of his credibility despite the statement change.

My response to the defence's attack on his statement was simple.

"Mr. Wilde is a respected man. He isn't violent, and he tries to avoid confrontation as the evidence I have shown today clarifies. You can go all the way back to high school where he was horrifically bullied for years because he wouldn't fight back. Mr. Wilde will tell you he was taunted in his early twenties and often called homosexual because of his mild nature and his avoidance of male chauvinistic behaviour. He didn't want another reason to be abused, hence why he didn't mention Mr. Carlton's unwanted advances until he absolutely had to. The advances were no more than a glance over the urinal and a throwaway comment."

After hearing witness testimony we adjourned for lunch.

I casually checked my phone; it was an automatic thing in the twenty-first century. I wasn't expecting to see anything in particular, but I absolutely did not predict a missed call from *Brooke*.

My stomach dropped all the way to my feet. My body should've been used to it by now; the fight or flight response was on alert. My heart raced, and my instinct for self-preservation kicked into focus.

I'd had no contact with Brooke since our conversation at Beth's apartment almost two weeks ago. I'd blocked her phone number on my return home from Japan. Did it feel slightly childish? Yes, but survival instincts took over, and I had to find a way to get through my first week back.

I lasted three days; that's all I could manage.

If anything, it made me think about her more, so my plan failed miserably; it always did where Brooke was concerned. I told myself I had to be available. What if she needed to contact me in an emergency? If only I was the person she'd contact, no that'd probably be Takara— I wasn't bitter.

Seeing her number grace my screen threw me. The Wilde case had been a welcome distraction the moment I touched base back in London. If I said I'd barely had time to think about her I'd be lying, but I was as busy as I could be. Throwing myself into work was no long-term solution, but it allowed me to function with some normality, which I desperately needed.

A tap on my shoulder pulled me from my trance.

"Are you okay? I shouted your name twice," Paula said.

"Sorry, I was distracted." I fumbled with my phone, placing it back in my briefcase. I could text her later. I was sure it'd be nothing important. I could act mellow and easy-going; it didn't have to be a big deal. As soon as the words entered my brain's atmosphere, I knew I'd be anything but easy-going. I was embarrassingly the opposite of easy-going when it came to Brooke.

"You look flustered," she observed.

I gave her my biggest fakest smile. "I'm fine."

"You sure?" Paula questioned.

I nodded, unconvincingly.

"You're doing amazing in there by the way. The defence doesn't stand a chance." Paula beamed.

"Good. I'm glad you think so. I'm just concerned they might have added something into evidence that I'm unaware of. It seems a little too easy right now. Don't you think?"

"I don't think so."

"You can't be sure though. I have contradicting evidence for everything they're putting forward. Everything I say is throwing their case into jeopardy."

I should've been smug, but I was sceptical, and Mr. Wilde's case fast became the second thing on my mind.

"I know you; you've combed through that evidence within an inch of its life, as you always do, and you've got Baron eating out of the palm of your hand." Paula winked. "She likes her a bit of Holly Garland." I thought she was about to age backwards fifty years and start singing, *Baron and Garland sitting in a tree*, thankfully she didn't.

"I don't know about that."

"She's sustained your every objection. At one point I think I saw her lips move. I'm not saying she smirked, but her lips became less of a straight line." Paula chuckled.

"Must've been trapped wind," I jested. Judge Baron doesn't smile; it's one of those things just beyond the bounds of possibility.

The adjournment was over. I was summoned back into the courtroom for closing statements. They were my favourite part of court proceedings. I brought the case home, left the jury with no doubt about their decision, and presented an argument so indisputable it made their job easy and mine successful.

I composed myself and flicked through my notes. Most of it was memorised, and I liked my closing statements to be a little off the cuff, so I felt comfortable, but my mind was on something else.

Regardless, I had a job to do—

"Members of the jury, thank you for your attention on this important case." I pointed at the defence.

"Mr. Carlton wasn't beaten within an inch of his life. The twelve of you weren't beaten that night, and neither was I, but my client Mr. Wilde was. You've seen the evidence. You've seen the X-rays and the CCTV of the brutal attack. The attacker Mr. Carlton might not look scary to you now, sat with a suit on, his beard trimmed, his doting family watching from the stands, but this man..." I turned to face Mr. Carlton and continued, "followed the defendant outside into a dark parking lot with only one intention, to cause grievous bodily harm. The evidence has shown beyond a reasonable doubt that my client was attacked unprovoked. The defence are pushing self-defence through false accusations with no evidence or merit other than a coerced testimony from a witness with zero credibility."

I paused to let that sink in, catching my breath and steadying myself for the next part.

"What you witnessed on that footage was pure rage. It shows a man out of control, a man so overcome with emotion he couldn't control himself. What you might ask is, why? Why was he so angry? The defence stated it's because he was sexually assaulted in the urinal minutes before, but the evidence is stacked against them. The CCTV footage shows a man overcome with emotion because he was afraid of being exposed. Did Mr. Carlton mean to hurt Mr. Wilde so severely? Potentially not, but he did. That cannot be denied. Allow me to take a few minutes to summarise all the evidence for you once again."

I took the jury on a quick whistle stop tour of the trial and the evidence, picking apart the defence's theory and driving home the desired verdict.

"Finally, I appreciate your patience, and I thank you for your time. My client is a victim, and he deserves better. Anything but a guilty verdict against Mr. Carlton would be a tragedy."

I unbuttoned my suit jacket and took a seat next to Mr. Wilde.

My job was done.

It was just another day in court. I had learnt to detach myself over the years. The more complex, and challenging the cases became, the more I emotionally disconnected myself in order to do my job. I wished it was that easy when it came to Brooke.

*

It was 5 p.m. The sun was shining, and the trial had gone without too many unexpected surprises. I liked a curveball occasionally. Sometimes thinking on my feet allowed me to excel; you either thrived under pressure or you didn't. Luckily, pressure had served me well so far.

I parted ways with Mr. Wilde; he was extremely gracious and thankful for my support.

"I'm only doing my job," I said.

"Yes, but you're good at it. Let's hope we never have to meet again, but if I need a lawyer you'll be the first person I call." He shook my hand firmly.

I was only doing my job. That part was true, but there was more to it. I always performed my duties to the best of my ability, regardless of who I was defending, but a small part of me pushed through that extra hour before I fell to sleep or woke up an hour earlier than normal to prepare when I believed in the character of the person I was defending.

Outside the courthouse Mr. Carlton's family scowled my way before climbing into their blacked-out Range Rover. I couldn't imagine the marriage would last much longer after the trial. Even if by some miracle he didn't get convicted, the evidence regarding his extramarital affairs would certainly give his wife some food for thought. I wasn't proud of breaking up a marriage, but on the flip side, there was a certain force generated by a person's actions and I liked to call that *karma*.

Paula came running out after me, seemingly to warn me about something.

"Holly. Wait. I need to tell—" She stopped dead in her tracks. "Never mind." She smirked and went in the opposite direction.

"Paula? What the hell?" I tutted to myself. She pulled stupid stunts all the time, but this was a new one. Did she want me to chase her? The lines in my forehead seeped deeper than they had all day.

She turned, smirked at me and flicked her head in the direction of the carpark.

"What?" I mouthed, conscious there were now ten people between us, so shouting would've been inappropriate.

I turned to see what, or should I say *who*, she'd been referring to.

"Is that?" I whispered.

It can't be.

*

I froze.

The hairs on my arms stood on end.

My breathing turned to short sharp spurts.

The sun was shining on a female figure leaning against the wall across the carpark. The glare made her features difficult to see, but I would recognise her anywhere. The sun bounced off her blonde hair giving it a sharp healthy shine. She wore long white high-waisted trousers that elongated her figure splendidly, combined with a yellow vest top and a denim jacket slung over the wall beside her, she looked amazing.

She gave off a European tourist look, like she'd just stepped off a plane from Milan. Her bronzed skin glistened in the sunlight. She was a picture of perfection. She didn't wave immediately, which made me question if it was her or if she was a figment of my imagination. It wouldn't be the first time I'd imagined a similar scenario.

I wandered down the steps slowly, taking each at a snail's pace. The slower I walked the less chance she would disappear and the more time I had to prepare for the encounter.

Brooke was here, in London. She stood in front of the crown court, casually leaning against a wall like she belonged, like this was a regular occurrence for her.

Why?

I passed through the parking lot. I was close enough now to see the corner of her mouth lift into a charming smile. She pulled her jacket from the wall and walked three steps, closing the gap between us to arm's length.

"Hi," she said softly.

"Hi."

I raised my eyebrows, unable to contain the shock at seeing her. "What are you doing here?"

"I did call." She shrugged.

"Is that what that was? How did you know where to find me?" Then it clicked. "Paula?"

Brooke nodded before sheepishly playing with the buttons on her jacket.

"She gave me a mouthful about how stupid I was for leaving you, then a long disapproving chat about my choices in Japan, but she agreed flying back to London to try and win you back was the best idea I've ever had." Brooke's gaze darted around the parking lot.

Wait, what did she say?

"You came back for me?" I asked softly.

My body was in disbelief. I'd gone from the highs of a strong day in court to this euphoric feeling I couldn't describe.

"Yes." The sun made the freckles on her nose stand out. The brown of her eyes looked golden.

"Why?" I whispered.

"You know why."

My briefcase was weighing me down, so I dropped it to the floor. Brooke took the opportunity to grab my hand.

"I love you, Holly. I was naive to think I could forget that. Leaving you was the hardest thing I've ever had to do. When I saw you again all those feelings came rushing back. They were more overwhelming than when I left you. It became clear to me how big a mistake I'd made."

Brooke placed her denim jacket on top of my bag and reached to cup my cheek. "I'm sorry for everything."

"What about Takara?"

"Me and Takara were never serious. It was pretty much done when I told her I'd always been in love with someone else."

Is this a dream?

I reached out and touched her arm, her shoulder, her neck.

She was real.

"What about your dad?" I cringed. I knew the answer would involve another lie. What tale had she told him this time?

"He'll probably never talk to me again, or at least not for a long time, but that's his problem now."

My eyes widened. "Wait, what? You told him the truth?"

"How else was I going to justify moving back to London? Saying I loved my job as a paralegal just wasn't going to cut it." She smirked.

"You're moving back?" I said in a low almost inaudible tone. "Where? How? Why do I feel like I'm dreaming?"

I reached forwards and touched a strand of hair lying across her chest.

"Have I died and gone to heaven?"

She looked me dead in the eye; her eyes squinted slightly to avoid the sun's glare. The expression created tiny little creases in the corners of her eyes that made her even more appealing.

"No, this is so much better than heaven," she whispered.

The palm of Brooke's hand fell from my face to my neck and stopped on my chest.

"I haven't figured out a lot of things yet, but I would prefer to talk about that later. Right now, all I want to do is—"

Before she finished her sentence I pressed my lips hard against hers. Years' worth of anguish and sorrow poured out into that kiss. She wrapped her hands around my back as I pulled her in closer. My hands ran through her hair. I felt her body close in on mine, and the world around us fell away.

When I pulled away her eyes remained closed. Our foreheads pressed together. I could smell her; the sweet aroma of a body spray unknown to me, but she smelt like summer. It was a coconut and citrus combination.

A kiss was never just a kiss. If I was asked to describe our kiss, I would say it was simple. It was a million moments, a million thoughts, a million wants, dreams and desires all coming to fruition. It was two years' worth of memories crashing together to create a few seconds of bliss.

It was a light bulb moment.

In one big "ah-ha" everything fell into place, and life suddenly made sense.

CHAPTER SEVENTEEN

A week later I strolled into my living room. It looked the same as it always did: neutral tones, the blinds drawn, and the TV playing reruns of *The Simpsons*. The only new addition in recent months was the trolley table that housed a selection of wines.

My first intention was to have it for show. I'd seen something similar in a house magazine at work. It was a subscription Ashleigh signed up for but couldn't figure out how to cancel, so the magazine ended up mixed in with my mail.

The trolley table held a bottle of red, a half bottle of white, two glasses, and a small bowl of peanuts. The sight was similar to a few weeks prior, but if it were a game of spot the difference, the second picture revealed two glasses instead of the usual one. I was no longer drinking alone.

The situation felt surreal. I took a moment to take it all in. I looked at Brooke in her little grey pyjama set with her sun-kissed arms and legs sprawled across my sofa. Her hair was messy, tied up in a bun atop her head with a giant grey scrunchy that matched her outfit. Her hair fell across her neck and shoulders in certain places; it almost looked posed, but I knew it wasn't.

Brooke's beauty came from her effortless approach to everything in life. She managed to pay no attention to her appearance but look like she had. I didn't understand how that was possible. It baffled me.

She threw her head back and a fit of laughter filled the air. It was a response to something funny Bart Simpson said, but I wasn't paying attention to the TV. My eyes were fixated on her: the dimples in her cheeks, the crinkles on her nose, the infectious smile I had longed to be around for so long.

She reached for the wine glass and took a small sip and then another. I didn't avert my gaze; she was my daydream I didn't want disturbed.

"What are you staring at you idiot?" She laughed.

"You."

Her cheeks flushed.

"Stop it." Brooke said shyly.

The intensity didn't revert to normal right away. My eyes focused vividly on her. Stray thoughts were roaming around my head. I felt disconnected for a moment and allowed myself to process what was in front of me. I picked out the thought that screamed louder than the rest.

"Move in with me?"

The words escaped my mouth too quickly.

Silence.

I watched Brooke's hand drop from her face in slow motion. *Well done. Now you've scared her away.*

"What?"

She placed her wine glass on the table and pulled her knees to her chest. She manoeuvred her body into a poised and upright position. There was no choice but to commit.

"Move in with me?"

"Seriously?" Brooke asked.

"Yes. Why not?"

She patted the seat to her right, and I moved in beside her.

"That's a big decision to make. Are you sure?" she questioned, reaching for the sleeve of my T-shirt and twiddling the hem between her fingers.

"Would you say yes?"

She nodded. No hesitation. My heart rate eased.

"Well, you've been here with me for the past week. I've loved coming home to you. I've loved making tea with you. I've loved watching TV with you. I've loved... y'know... doing other things with you." I smirked.

"Naughty." She grinned.

"It's everything I've ever wanted. It's a no brainier for me."

It made perfect sense.

"Okay." She smirked.

"What?" I asked.

"Okay."

"Say it a bit louder. I can't hear you." I tickled her stomach, prodding at her playfully.

"OKAY. I'LL MOVE IN WITH YOU," she yelled.

"Jesus, okay, okay, you can move in." I winked.

She grabbed my hands and pulled me towards her. The soft warmth of her lips touched mine, and once again I was transported to a dream-like state. A few months ago, I would never have thought Brooke would come back to me. I feared I'd never see her again. I dreamt I would, but I don't think I truly believed it.

Now, here she was kissing me, hugging me, tugging at my hair playfully, nibbling on my neck, and inhaling my scent, and strangely rubbing her nose against my neck like she was performing some sort of animal greeting. Coming from her it was the cutest damn thing I'd ever experienced.

"Why do you always smell so good?" She breathed me in. I didn't move. I fell backwards onto the sofa, leaving my neck exposed as she climbed on top like a vampire seductively stalking its prey, except a lot less scary and more humorous.

My hands searched for her arms and pulled her closer; her whole body shook as she belly laughed. The sensitivity of her underarms only made me target them more.

She softly bit my neck, making chomping sounds that clarified the vibe was less sexual and more good-natured.

"So . . ." Brooke leant against my chest looking me directly in the eyes.

"So . . ." I replied.

"I guess we're doing this then?" Brooke grinned.

"I guess we are." I brushed my fingertips across her cheek.

"I love you," she confessed.

"Not as much as I love you."

She tutted and rolled, propelling her body to the left hurtling towards the floor and taking me with her.

We were a pile of tangled limbs playfully giggling like children. In a world full of wonderous sights, there was nowhere else I'd rather be.

EPILOGUE

Eighteen Months Later
New Year's Eve

"It'll just be a few twinkly lights and balloons," Brooke said.

Three hours earlier I'd been summoned to leave the apartment for a visit to Beth's house and an afternoon spent with my adorable baby niece, Willow. I welcomed that part with open arms, but what I would return to scared the life out of me.

Beth moved back to London in the summer and it was the highlight of my year. She and Ren found an adorable townhouse on the outskirts of London. She started work as an English teacher in a school nearby, and Ren worked at some swanky corporation in the centre of London. I got to see my best friend on a regular basis and fully live out my cool Aunt Holly fantasy.

Willow was yet to turn one, and she loved me more than she loved anyone else. That was a fact. We had the best games of peekaboo. She especially loved it when I'd gather her in my arms and bounce around like a monkey from one room to the next. It was the small things, and I vowed to take full advantage of them before she turned eighteen and wanted nothing to do with me or Beth.

The time spent with Willow had softened my core. It made me rethink my values and reassess what I wanted from life. Children were now officially on the cards. *Gulp.*

Brooke came bounding around the corner from the living room as I stepped through the front door.

"Hold on! I have one more thing to finish. Wait there." She was forceful with her request, so I stood in the entrance hall adhering to her demand.

The entrance hall table had been turned into a confetti bar according to the sign. There were five different plastic bowls; three of them contained confetti, in pink silver and white, which I could only assume was the theme of the party. The fourth bowl housed enough party poppers to get the whole street involved, and the fifth bowl had clear circle shaped lollipops with pink bows and pink writing that said—

I looked closer.

A Brolly NYE Party 2023.

"What do you think?" Brooke appeared at my left and planted a quick kiss on my cheek. "Do you love the lollipops?" She grinned.

"Brolly?"

"Yeah, as in Brooke and Holly. I toyed with a few messages, but it's a play on words; instead of jolly I used Brolly; I think it's cute."

"Interesting." I laughed.

Never once had she referred to us as "Brolly". Paula would have a field day with that one. *Who do you think you are with your own nickname, Brangelina?* I could hear her already. She hadn't quite moved on from their untimely demise.

Brooke laced her fingers with mine and pulled me towards the living room.

"Anyway, why is it Brolly and not Holoke? Or Hooke?" I asked.

"Because they sound ridiculous." Brooke laughed.
And Brolly doesn't?

I stopped by the large vintage floor mirror in the hall. It had fairy lights draped from head to toe. It gave off a warm glow and almost a magical feel. Never had I ever thought of anything in my apartment as magical.

"I like that."

"I thought you might because it's the least extravagant thing I've done."

The heavy wooden door to the living room had a silver *Happy New Year* sign sagging from one side to the next and about twenty paper fans and stars creating a symmetrical festive feeling.

The far wall that held the TV was covered in clock themed balloons in a variety of colours. The coffee table had been moved over by the window. It was covered in pink glitter, a giant cocktail glass display, and mini disco balls. Brooke managed to hang a giant disco ball from the ceiling too; I almost hit my head on it.

"This is the dance floor." She'd removed the large rustic beige rug we'd purchased a few months ago and used a strip of lights to outline a square and segregate that part of the floor from the rest.

"That's a genius idea." I had to hand it to her, she had a knack for party planning.

"I know. I thought so too. I enquired about a portable dance floor, but it was quite pricey, and I did already massively overspend on alcohol." She mouthed the word "oops", in the most adorable way.

Out the corner of my eye, I saw a large garish display. It felt like it was closing in on me like a tissue paper covered giant. I had a feeling the car sized box that got delivered the week before had something to do with it.

"Wow."

It was a genuine response.

"It's amazing, right?"

"Erm . . . yeah. It's colourful."

"The theme I've gone for is disco glitz. I saw it in a magazine. What do you think?"

"I think there's a lot of colour, glitter, and confetti all over my apartment." I was going to be hoovering it up for months to come.

"It's actually our apartment now, and people are going to love it!"

The wall was covered in long streams of paper tissue. Each layer was a different colour, but they didn't stray too far from the pink palette. There was a large balloon arch stretching from one side of the wall to the other; it was made from a mix of pink and white balloons, some small, some large, and the odd one here and there with New Year's themed slogans and dates. It was impressive.

"Did you make that yourself?"

"The balloon arch?"

I nodded.

"God no. I can't even tie balloons without hurting my finger. I paid a woman." She grinned.

Brooke had a *woman* for everything these days: a woman to clean the oven, a woman to do her eyebrows, a woman to supply her with candles and diffusers, and now a woman to do balloon arches.

The display was impressively finished off with a fluorescent pink light up sign in the middle that spelt out the word, *Hooray*.

"This is the photo wall." She gestured towards the tripod set up in front. "You put your phone in here, turn the light on and voilà."

She set the ten-second timer on her phone and pulled me behind the camera.

"Smile."

She ran back around, clicked the timer again, and launched herself into my arms, showering me with kisses.

"One more." She hit the timer again, took her position at my side, and pinched my bum for good measure.

"Why is nothing flashing," I mumbled through the side of my smile.

"Because this one's on video."

Brooke stepped back and looked up into my eyes. I watched in slow motion as she bent down slowly onto one knee.

"Brooke, what are you doing?"

There was a look on her face I'd never seen before. There was a longing in her eyes. I could sense her nerves as her hands began to shake. She looped her hand behind her back and brought forward a small brown box tightly grasped in her fingertips.

"Oh My God." My mouth gaped.

"Holly Garland . . ."

"Yes," I said eagerly.

"When I tell you every morning that you are *it* for me, I mean it. There is no one else in this world I would give up my whole life for. There is no one else I would move across the world for with a suitcase and no plan. You are my once-in-a-lifetime, and you are my forever."

Her eyes began to fill and so did mine.

"Do you remember, in the letter you wrote me? You said one day you hoped I'd be content with my life. Maybe I'd even be married with children, and you hoped I would remember the time we spent together and smile at the memories. Well, that wasn't possible for me. It was never going to be anyone but you. I will never want that life with anyone but you. Here I am today, down on one knee, which wasn't something I saw as a kid when I dreamt of a wedding, and ponies, and dresses. As little girls we are often programmed to think Ken is destined to be with Barbie, but what if Barbie wants to marry another Barbie?"

"Barbie should always do what's right for her." I chuckled through the tears.

"Exactly. Holly Garland, I love you. I have loved you since the moment you looked up from your desk and asked me what my favourite colour was. Will you please make me the happiest girl on this planet and agree to spend the rest of your life with me? Marry me?"

"Of course I will marry you."

Brooke leapt to her feet and placed the gold-banded single solitaire diamond on my finger. It fit perfectly.

"I knew you wouldn't want anything too extravagant, so I went for a single diamond. I hope you like it."

"I love it, and I love you."

I cupped her face with my hands and kissed her tenderly. The taste of salty pretzels was still on her lips from her inability to avoid the snack station.

How did I get so lucky?

I was engaged.

I had a fiancée.

*

I held my arm outstretched in front of my body with my palm open and my fingers spread. The second finger in from the left took all my attention. The shine from the disco ball in the lounge reflected off the diamond and caused it to twinkle like a star in the night's sky. I'd been ready for over an hour, which was remarkably early by my standards, so there was nothing for me to do other than admire it.

"Hey you," Brooke purred in my ear. "Have you just been sat staring at your ring?" She chuckled.

"You're damn right I have."

She came around the other side of the chair to face me from the front. "Are you ready to do this?" Her face turned cold.

"I think so." I nodded. "Things went well last time, right? I think he'll be okay."

"I hope so."

I lifted Brooke's hand and kissed each finger with a full-lipped peck. "I will make sure you have a shiny diamond on this finger soon; I promise."

"There's no rush." Brooke smized.

"There is! I want people to know you're taken. Done. Completely off the market. Forever." I winked.

"Sounds like a dream," she whispered against my lips. The doorbell interrupted our moment. It was showtime.

"Here we go." Brooke tucked her hair behind her left ear and patted down her silver sparkling dress. She was poised.

I heard the door close and Brooke walked in followed by her brother, Tom, and her father, Robert. His presence put me on edge, but we'd made progress in recent months. He'd returned to the UK on a surprise visit a year prior with an air of regret. He told Brooke he would try to accept her "lifestyle"—I hated it when people called it a lifestyle, but it wasn't my place. He was back for a week over New Year's. He'd arrived in London the day before.

Robert held out his hand. "Holly, it's nice to see you again." He smiled, and it seemed genuinely sincere.

"You too, Robert. How was the flight?"

"Long." He sighed. "However, it gave me the opportunity to pre-order something for my arrival." He pulled two small thin black boxes from the inside of his jacket pocket. "I don't know what you kids are into these days, but I hope you like them."

Is he pranking me? I half expected to find a basic biro pen in the box, or a twig. There was no way Robert Jacobs was buying me a gift from Frost of London. I cautiously opened the box. Inside was a gold tennis bracelet.

Is this real? It would be rude to ask, but it didn't look cheap.

"Dad, this is beautiful."

Brooke had the same but in silver.

"It's so nice, thank you so much, but you didn't have to." I said.

Robert put his hand up in protest. "I don't want to hear it. It's Christmas, and I wanted to treat my daughter, and her . . . girlfriend."

He'd already sent Brooke a substantial amount of money for her Christmas present, but this gesture was all together unbelievable. It was the first time I'd heard him refer to me as her girlfriend, and it felt like the biggest step in the right direction.

Tom didn't say much at all. He was, according to Brooke, pissed off he'd had to leave his girlfriend in Tokyo to fly back and see his sister. I can imagine his dad left him with no choice, which was rather funny to watch now that Brooke was no longer under the same spell.

"Actually Dad . . ."

I glared at her. Alarm and panic spread across my face top to bottom.

What are you doing?

"Holly isn't my girlfriend anymore." She reached for my hand and held it up. "We're engaged."

I looked at Robert.

He looked at me.

Tom observed from the sidelines with a wry smile.

I wanted to turn into a disco ball and explode in a shower of glitter. It was *not* how I foresaw the night starting.

Brooke didn't release my hand. There was no questioning her confidence or her ability to stand up for herself where her father was concerned anymore.

I half expected Robert to turn and leave, but he took a moment to compose himself. The silence was uncomfortable. Then he smiled.

He actually *smiled*.

"It's a beautiful ring. Similar to the first ring I got your mum actually." He nodded towards the bracelet in my other hand. "Looks like gold was the right choice for you, Holly, it matches your new ring."

Was this whole thing a prank?

"Erm, yeah, it does. Thank you."

"Can your old man give you both a hug?" Robert extended his arms.

Brooke looked up at me. She was as confused by his reaction as I was. She nodded. Before I had a chance to say anything, I felt the itchy wool of Robert's suit jacket against my right cheek and the roughness of his day-old stubble against my left.

This was weird.

I placed my hand on his back and was conscious of feeling like a melon being squeezed to death by a bear. I'd seen it first-hand while camping in Japan—bears liked melon, apparently. I felt Brooke's hand slide over the top of mine. She was still holding my ring finger as our shoulders crushed together.

"Okay, Dad. I think that's enough hugging," Brooke said light-heartedly. He eased his grip and took a step back.

"I'm really happy for you both."

Is he dying?

I wasn't proud of it being my first thought, but I don't think anyone could blame me for thinking it. Who was this man? And what had he done with Robert Jacobs?

"Thanks Dad; that means so much to me."

Tom nodded in our direction. "Congrats, lovebirds." He said insincerely.

Brooke scowled at him.

"Can I get you both a drink?" Brooke asked.

"Whiskey neat please, sweetheart." Robert turned towards me; his usual stare unnerved me, but it was softer somehow. "Holly, why don't you show me the apartment? I'd love to see."

Gulp.

This is too much.

"Erm, yeah, sure."

I'd only ever been around Robert when Brooke was present. When he'd come to London a year prior, he took us to dinner. He paid for us to attend the opera. He'd even provided Brooke with his American Express card so we could both get new outfits. The words spoken were few and far between, but he'd shown interest in my career and my life outside of being his daughter's girlfriend. Since then, he'd called Brooke once a week, just to check in, and the dark cloud that had surrounded the whole situation for a long time seemed to be gone with the wind.

Brooke smiled softly.

This was important to her. It was everything she'd dreamed of, and I wanted that for her and for us.

*

"Did Beth just slut drop in front of your dad?" Brooke burst out laughing.

"Yes, yes she did." I pointed towards my best friend and mouthed the words, "I'm watching you." Beth was in her element. Her sparkly gold floor-length dress was pulled up slightly at her knees, as she made the necessary room to shake her backside. Ren leant against the wall in the corner entertaining my mum in conversation and shaking his head occasionally at Beth's extravagant dance moves.

She stuck her tongue out in response. It was a rare baby-free night, and she was taking full advantage. My dad was a good sport. It wasn't the first time Beth had coerced him onto the dancefloor over the years.

"It's like watching Margot Robbie twerk on Mr. Bean." Brooke laughed. She passed me another glass of champagne. I wasn't keeping track, and I couldn't work out if the room turning slightly was to do with the disco ball or the alcohol.

"Are you saying my dad looks like Mr Bean?" I reached my arm around her back and pulled her in at the waist.

"I'm saying he's as stiff as Mr. Bean." She had a point. His signature dance move was a combination of the two-step and a weird arm movement I liked to call the spin cycle.

"It's true." I laughed.

Tom had been surprisingly pleasant all evening. He clearly had a crush on Beth, which I found hilarious. He tried to steal a glance her way whenever Ren wasn't around, and he went out of his way to provide her with another drink.

"Beth told me your brother hit on her at the buffet station."

"Why am I not shocked? What did he say?"

I could barely repeat the cheesy chat up line.

"Oh god, tell me," Brooke insisted.

"He said, and I quote 'My favourite dish at this buffet is you'."

"No, he didn't?" Brooke's mouth gaped.

"Yep." I smirked.

"I'm going to kill him." She scowled in his direction.

"It's all fun and games." I chuckled. Beth could handle just about anything. Tom flirting wouldn't even phase her.

Robert was talking to my aunt over by the *Hooray* sign. The fluorescent pink caused his white shirt to look a baby pink colour. He'd been working the room all night and introducing himself to everyone; he was even cooperative when we spent ten minutes posing for group photos. I liked to be as optimistic as the next person, but I'd been taught quite stringently in my line of work to air on the side of caution, and Robert's personality transplant did concern me.

"Your dad seems in good spirits." I smiled.

"This is the side of him I hoped you'd see one day. He's not all bad; he just made some bad choices." Brooke leant her head against my shoulder. Maybe she was right; maybe this was the fresh start we needed.

"Do you think he likes me?" I asked. My insides curled as I said the words. The sad thing was, I desperately wanted his approval.

"I think he does, and I think he will grow to love you because it's near impossible not to." Brooke looked up, pursing her mouth for me to plant a quick peck on her freshly glossed lips.

"You love me, don't you?" I teased.

"More than you will ever know."

The wind slashed spots of rain across the window, but nobody was talking about the weather. The topics of conversation flowed freely. The music set the tone. The volume reverted from high to low every time the randomised New Year's Eve playlist threw out a banger that nobody was fond of. They often came at the appropriate time when everyone was due a refill and a bite of buffet food for dancing energy.

The dark green chair in the corner was being used as Paula's prop, as she started what looked like some sort of *Moulin Rouge* routine. A lawyer from work named Steve started to play the air guitar even though it was musically inappropriate for the song. My mum tried but failed to get Ren to dance whilst my friend Jake was getting—Robert to do a shot?

I blinked twice. The odour of champagne made my nose tingle. If the countdown wasn't a mere ten minutes away, I would have stood outside in the pouring rain just to check I wasn't hallucinating. The scenes unfolding warmed my heart. The room was filled with all our favourite people, and they were getting along, despite contrasting personalities, age gaps, and political differences. Every person in the room was making the effort to be in the moment, to be present, and to be *happy*.

"Do you remember the first time you ever said you loved me?" I asked.

"Like I could forget."

"Do you remember what else you said?" I quizzed.

She shook her head, waiting for me to enlighten her.

"You said, 'one day we will get to celebrate New Year's together with both our families'." I smiled. "At one stage I had a hard time believing that would ever be possible, but here we are."

"We made it." Brooke winked.

"I will never take this for granted." I clinked my glass to Brooke's. "I'm the happiest I have ever been, and I have you to thank for that."

I wasn't sure I would ever be able to put into words what it felt like to have my soulmate ripped from my grasp. A dull ache and years of endless monotony were my torment whilst I waited, hoped, and prayed she would come back to me. I lost faith on some of my darker days. I cursed every god I didn't believe in. It was like living in a world without colour, and then, suddenly, she returned to me, and I was seeing the world through a different pair of eyes. The world didn't make sense without Brooke by my side.

"This is a dream come true," Brooke expressed.

In that moment, as the countdown commenced, the cheers of my family and the loud chanting of my friends filled the room. There was so much joy in the faces of the people I loved the most, but amongst the chaos there was only Brooke; This was the paralyzing culmination, my triumph.

She chose me, above all others, and in return I will always *choose* her.

Thank you for reading *Choose Us*. I hope you enjoyed it.

Want to stay updated with news about my books?

Follow me on Instagram: **@nss_writings**

Follow me on Twitter: **@NicoleSkillen**

Like me on Facebook: **NicoleSpencerSkillen**

And if you have a moment, please take the time to review *Choose Us*. I would be eternally grateful.

Thank you once more for your support, and I hope we meet again between the pages of another book.

ABOUT THE AUTHOR

Nicole Spencer-Skillen is a bestselling author of Sapphic Romance novels and a die-hard LA Lakers fan. She is incredibly passionate about writing novels with relatable, funny, and emotionally compelling LGBT+ characters.

Born and raised in Lancashire, England, she has aspirations of surfing rooftop bars and ice-skating in Central Park, whilst living out her dream career in New York City.

Printed in Great Britain
by Amazon